JUSTICE AND THE LAW

BY JIM DENSON

CONTENTS

PREFACE

An idea has flickered in the chasm of my mind from time to time. An outlaw spinning a pistol on one finger, and drawing his second pistol with the other all the while having a menacing smile. A young man the manifestation of purity trying to stay clean in a filthy land when his peers may be just as bad as the criminals they hunt. Abstract ideas and deep textual lines making one stop and think twice. All this comes from I don't know where. This is the work of roughly five years off and on. Starting from a short story in college for one of the best teachers I've ever had. A true feminist who loved man still, she never destroyed my delicate penmanship by pointing out all the obvious grammar errors. No, she wanted to just hear the story and help me push it out. Thank you Max Stewart, and also to Dr. Robert Peluso, a wise teacher who walks in the same steps as Socrates. With the knowledge and skill of a Roman, he has taught me of August Wilson, Chinua Achebe, the masterpiece "Heart of Darkness" by Joseph Conrad as well as many other great stories by great authors in addition to cherished life lessons. Thank you to the House of Orsini who are my brothers, sisters, mothers, fathers, sons, daughters, and grandparents who accepted me with nothing but love. A bit of the country essence in writing this book may be attributed to them in our many days of drinking moonshine and drunken nights of laughter broke as a joke as we loved life. They took me in when I was beaten and bloody laying in the street on the road to Damascus. May the tribe of Denson forever come to your aid in battle. My grandmother Gwen who I hope to name my daughter after some day is probably the only person to have faith in me. Thank you as well to Professor James Yamber of ITT-Tech, a wise old Scott teaching those of lessor when he could easily be teaching at an Ivy League school. Thank you to Jon Amakawa my Sensei, who was the first to tell me I was really smart when I didn't believe it. He took what some would call a thug and purified and sharpened the old blade turning it into a work of art. And there are many others to be thankful for with God being one and too many others to name. Before we get right into the book, the muse of my father James Denson Sr. flows through from him to me. He was a writer and now I am as well. He may not have been published (yet), but it is to him that I owe my gifts. Rest with the ancestors, father. And now my first book ever which I hope will not be my last, Justice and the Law.

CHAPTER 1

An open glen in the wilderness the Sun shining his rays on God's creation. A long snake breathing fire and smoke slithers through, cutting the plain in half as a train approaches. On an overstretching cliff, one could see five shadows sitting on horseback as gloom and death swirl on winds over them. Four go left while one goes right. Inside the front of this train there is the conductor and his coal shoveling assistant. In the next cart, the train staff quarters, then we come to first class which holds some of the most prominent north easterners and their wives or mistresses for the first time in the west. The next cart is the same. After that, the coach cart. Going past the coach cart, one can see a cart with a firmly-locked door restricting access to a large cast iron safe. Six men of Jefferson Security Service, two of them loaded up with rifles (one holding a double-barrel shotgun while the other three carry two six-shooters a piece) stand waiting. The next cart held two more men who were dressed in gray trench coats and carrying rifles like the other security men. These guards patrolled up and down the back to mid-carts which held the kitchen cart. Here, even the cooks were too afraid to look at the security men. Then we come to the final five carts which held passenger luggage, and the final two held four Jefferson Security men all with six-shooters bringing up the rear. The train's engine roared as it ate the coal it was fed. The train staff adhered to the needs of the first class while the cooks prepared the day's lunch.

"What's that?!" One cook stopped and shouted. "I didn't hear nothing," The other cook said, his mouth full of food. He was chubbier than the first and didn't look startled. "Naw Peerson, I heard something on the roof."

Peerson yelled, "Buck, you drinking that coon shine again. The devil himself isn't coming in here with these bastards, I hear these Jefferson boys isn't to be fooled wit ex bandits and runaway Calvary and such, keep quiet." "Tap Tap!" "See, you heard it Peerson." Peerson walked toward the door and opened it to peek up. "Probably some damn coon hauled off on the roof from that damn station." Just then a young black face appeared in front of him with a dark hat, large eyes, and a menacing smile. "You're half right," said the mysterious figure who then produced a black-gloved hand as he gripped the back of Chef Peerson' s neck and pulled his fat head then his pot-bellied body all the way through the open door and on to the rocks below, rolling and breaking several of the man's bones in the process no doubt. The young man then slid through the doorway and stood in front of Buck smiling, covered head to toe in black leather garments with a rather fancy patterned under vest. He quickly produced a magnum revolver, its black polished steel looked like it was made out of ebony steel and its ivory handles had skulls engraved on both sides of it with red eyes. He pointed it at Buck's head.

"I got two more of these and I don't won't to have to waste them on you, turn around and hands up dammit." Buck did as he was told and then two young men clinging to the side of the train climbed in. The first was a tall lad with sharp blue eyes and a slender face in a brown trench coat. A brown scarf covered most of his mouth and he pulled it down to speak, "Perfect as always, Moses." The second man had no scarf, young with a large beard fit for a seasoned gold miner. His clothing was tattered and his smell was more than foul. "Let's blow something up!" he shouted before opening his trench to produce a row of sticks of dynamite on his belt with two sawed off double-barreled shotguns in each holster. "Zeke, I'm not shitting you. No fuck ups on this one." Lawson, a tall and towering man, said. "Lawson, I'm good," Ezekiel replied. "Law times a wasting, delicious!" Moses said, shoving raspberry crepes in his mouth with his magnum still pointed at Buck's head. Lawson then grabbed Buck's shirt and spoke, "It's your lucky day. You get to decide if you're gonna live or die today."

Buck approached the mid-car with two security detail men in it trying not to shake as he pushed a dinner cart with a white cloth draped over it. One of the two security men asked, "What you doing boy, dinner ain't for an hour." Buck replied, "Someone in first class wants theirs now, you know how they get." The man exclaimed, "The hell with that! No one cuts through, let me ask the Chief." As soon as the man turned, the glass window shattered and he grabbed his chest and dropped to the ground. A man lying flat on his stomach on a cliff reloaded a bolt action rifle. Its scope was so long it looked more like a telescope, and it had so many lines etched in it that there seemed to be another language written on the rifle butt. Before the other guard could ask what was wrong, he dropped to his knees and fell face first. The echo was loud but far away as the man got up from the cliff-side, pushed his glasses closer to his face and sprung through the mountain top as if he were a goat.

"What's that?" someone cried in the next room. Then came the unmistakable sound of guns cocking. Buck, scared for his earthly flesh, turned to Law who was walking in and murmured, "you said you wouldn't kill me if I-" Thump! "You calling me a liar, Buck?" Moses smirked as he whipped the back of

Buck's head with his pistol. Buck crumpled and fell to the ground. "Check it out." Chief Dawson said to the other men. Just then, a figure appeared to the men through the door window. "That's Owen!" One of the men announced. He quickly went to open the door. Owen stood there, quiet with his head hanging. "What's wrong?" one of the other men asked, puzzled. Owen's body dropped to the floor and Law stood there with a silver magnum pistol. The pistol featured a handsome design with two angels on each side. Each of the angels had their wings aimed straight forward in a fashion reminiscent to the angels on top of the Ark of the Covenant. In a fluid motion without the slightest trace of hesitation, Law pointed at the man's head and pulled the trigger. A heavy silence fell as red blood splattered everywhere. No one moved in the room. Each of the men stood frozen. Law, not even flinching, turned and shot another man who was carrying a shotgun. He only winged the man in the arm so that he stumbled before diving into a booth on the side for cover like a fish jumping out of water to catch a fly. At this, all of the security men began pulling their guns up in slow motion towards Law. Moses slid through the door on his knees with two guns up blazing. Bullets of hellfire cut through two men's chest as if they were only made of homemade Amish butter. All at once, the two men dropped to the floor as if they had only been one man standing in front of a mirror. The injured man Law winged began firing at Law's booth with his shotgun. If only he could fully control the shotgun with just one arm. Law yelled for cover, but Moses had rolled in the booth across from him taking cover from the Chief and another man who continued shooting. Moses laughed while spinning a gun on one finger before reloading it. The man next to the Chief had a rifle in hand, he smirked and took aim at the nearly destroyed booth when a multitude of small corn-sized pellets too enumerable to count hit his large body. He was instantly lifted up off the ground and slammed against the back wall before falling to the floor in silence. Ezekiel stepped through the doorway emptying two shells at once from his double-barreled sawed off. The Chief's eyes widened at the sight of Ezekiel. Sweat running down his face, he shouted orders at his man to fall back. He quickly ran to unlock the door while his man covered him. He and his remaining man ran into coach where people were crying and shouting in a frenzy as they looked for ways to escape. When they saw the look on his face, the last remaining passengers in coach lost their pride and ran into first class for their lives. At this, the Chief got his guts back when he saw a steel table that he could use for cover. He flipped the table over while his man covered the door. He shouted, "You're done! We got the door covered and you're gonna be hit from your backside in a sec. I got the key to that there safe around my neck, so give up!"

The train rounded a large mountainous region above before rolling on towards the setting sun. An eerie quiet now fell on the train. The Chief wiped his forehead and dried his hand on his long gray mullet. "Where's my back up?" he murmured to himself. Just then, shots wrung out behind him. "Woo, get em boys!" he shouted. Four men pumped lead into the car containing the three outlaws who each ran for cover behind the carts. The Chief and his last man did the same, running from cover to cover as the shots fired loudly in the air like the sound of cracking popcorn. After about a minute of straight unloading the Chief yelled, "Stop! If anyone's alive in there, come out hands up!" It was quiet as a graveyard and a man from the back cart yelled, "Boss we going in!" The Chief motioned to his last man with his eyes and a nod, directing him to go in as well. The Chief stayed firmly put behind the table. The four men in the back cart walked closer to what was left of the door. There was so much smoke from dust that they could see nothing but faint outlines. The man walked closer and closer to the door riddled with bullet holes when a single stick of dynamite was tossed through the shattered window and rolled towards him, touching his foot with its lit wick. He ran towards the other exit but was blocked by the table. The last thing he saw was the Chief's back running into first class. The explosion launched the Chief into first-class and face-first into the middle aisle. The dynamite blew a hole in the train floor and the man exploded into pieces. The four men stopped right before they were to step through the open door and looked at each other in shock. 10 sticks of dynamite bundled together rolled into the room as one man approached the doorway. Paul, Moses, and Ezekiel ran through the next cart where pieces of that unfortunate soul were scattered about. Running full speed towards first class and jumping over the hole in the floor, all three of the young fools appeared with smiles on their faces as if playing a game. BOOM! The fireball reached heaven and separated the train leaving the snake severed in half. People fell to the ground gripping loved ones for dear life. Women, children and even some men started to cry.

Law stepped in through a cloud of smoke which settled like scarf around his neck. He walked proudly like a cat up to a bowl of milk as the other outlaws followed behind him. Before reaching for the Chief's collar and grabbing the key to the safe, he chuckled and said, "The Lord giveth and he taketh away." As he stood up, he noticed a beautiful woman being held by her husband. He approached, took her hand and kissed it. "Madam, if this fella does not tell you daily that your smile lights up his morning more than the Sun itself then leave him at once and come and find me here in New Palestine. You will never be taken for granted again." He then walked away in the silence. The woman was full of fear at first, but then his words made a slight smile and blush come over her. Moses was the last one to step out when he heard a clicking noise. It was the Chief who stood up. His clothes were splattered with blood. One of his eyes was swollen and he now had a gun pointed directly at the group of outlaws. "I know who yawl are!" He announced angrily. "God's Hand! You're outlaws, thieves, murderous young punks and I'm a send one of you boys to hell at least for my men." Moses turned slowly and pointed his finger at the Chief. "Tell you what. If you're fast enough to pull that trigger before I reach my gun, you can live." He glanced over at Ezekiel. "You hear me Zeke? " Zeke replied, "Yup." Moses and the Chief locked eyes. The passengers stared ahead, too scared to even whimper as they huddled together in their booths against the sidewalls. "Ready?" Moses asked. BANG! A window shattered and a projectile shattered the Chief's skull before smashing into the next window. On a cliff side, the young man reloaded his bolt action rifle and pressed his glasses closer to his face as he laid on his stomach. Moses smiled softly and said, "Not fast enough." He stepped away to meet the others and laughed as if there were many demons in him laughing together as well. A skinny fragile man in the crowd fainted from this sight. Zeke smiled at Moses and said, "Saved by the prophet Elijah again, huh?" As he walked away, Moses replied, "My faith is in money, bullets, vodka, and your brother's aim."

Law walked back two carts and opened the safe which housed 10,000 dollars in cash and twenty-five U.S. Mint gold bars equaling 1,000 a piece. "Load up boys, let's go." he said. The men did so and walked to where a hole had blown into the train. They climbed on the side with satchels of loot tied to them and saw their horses being led by one young man, traveling alongside the train the whole time. He held a machete holster on his back and rustled the horses at full speed as if he had done this many times before. It was Je'sus, the last member of the gang and a Mexican of conquistador descent. He brought the horses closer holding their bridles, and the three young train-robbers jumped on their horses and rode off with sacks of loot, hooting, yelling, whistling, and wildly screaming all the way into the mountain valley. The train traveled on smoking, on fire in half stature as it rode off into the west sunset.

CHAPTER 2

"**D**amn it Governor Damen. I'm going to have to pull all my business out of New Palestine because you and your forces can't stop five young bandits who think they're led by some God." Milton Jefferson was the cattle, bank, farm and whatever else mogul in New Palestine and he was furious. He paced the back patio of the Governor's mansion where he was spitting, slurring and cursing. Rightfully so, as he was constantly getting robbed by The Hand. But this was huge as he had brought a large chunk of his fortune to the west with what he thought was tight security. "Shit Governor, I'm a have to back up and leave. " This made the Governor lean in and take the cigar out of his mouth. "Listen Milton, we need you here in New Palestine. I promise within three months time you'll see all these boys hanging in the wind." Milton leaned back in his chair and replied, "All right three months, how you going to do this Gerald? " "Don't worry," the Governor replied. "I have a special team lined up. Men who get the law done no matter the price. In fact, here they are now. Come in gentlemen." Four large men in their late thirties to early forties appeared in the archway to the garden and started to approach. A younger man stepped in behind them. He was a strapping lad but very timid looking. "Milton, this is Marshall William Evans, Teddy Johnson, Patrick O'Connor, Dennis Fitzgerald and I don't know this young man." "He's not important," Teddy said disinterestedly. "His name is J.J. and he's just a little schoolboy translator we brought along for Engines, Mexicans, and to wash our undergarments. " This made all the men chuckle except for William and J.J. Teddy was short but extremely muscular and it was evident that JJ was afraid of him. William stepped forward to show who was in charge. "Hush up, Ted. " Teddy became quiet. William spoke, "His name is Jeremiah, and he's fresh from West Point where he graduated top of his class." "J.J. For short sir."

Jeremiah added timidly.

The other men turned heads and looked at the ground. Milton turned and looked at the Governor in silence. Then he spoke, "You know, there are only four of these guys plus some tender-foot kid. The Hand slaughtered twelve of my best men and you telling me these boys are going to stop them?" The Governor reached his hand out to point at the law men and spoke, "Mr. Jefferson these ain't no ordinary law men." He sat up in his chair confidently as a proud look came across his face. "These four men single-handedly shut down whole savage Indian tribes and a slave rebellion. They fought face to face against General Lee himself in the war. Now they're America's secret weapon, one that Lincoln can't ignore and gets the job done." He finished his statement by pounding his fist on the table. "Mr. Jefferson, three months and I'll have them boys for you. Hell, I'll stake my kingdom on it."

William and the other marshals loaded up at a barn on the edge of Damascus, New Palestine. Each man had kept their side revolvers and rifles on their horses. They seemed to look the same as they were all dressed the same with clean-shaven faces and the same weapons. Except William, he kept just one revolver on his side. The revolver's handle was engraved on both sides with a bald eagle with its talons stretched forth ready to grab its prey. "What's the kid touting, a Derringer two shoot or that too much?" Ted started to laugh. Dennis and Pat joined in his laughter. J.J. said nothing and just packed up his maps and supplies. William walked over and put his hand on his shoulder then spoke, "Come on boys, we got a train to catch."

On an old farm between Maysville and Old Elnero lay the current hideout of God's Hand for they constantly moved and never stayed in one place. Law, Moses, Elijah, Ezekiel, and Je'sus all sat at a table sipping whiskey and rolling tobacco (some wacky) and divided their plunder as they laughed like children playing a game in the backyard. "Wuuuuuu! What gang runs New Palestine?" Moses bellowed loudly. Drunk off the whiskey and Zeke's moonshine, he shouted at the top of his lungs, "The Hand!" "No, who's the richest gang in New Palestine?" interjected Zeke with one finger pointed up. He grinned and glanced around the table. "Heck, we could be even richer if we cut out Paul Lawson's fantasy guy in the sky." Elijah's sentence bathed the table in silence. "You calling me a thief?" Law replied, his cold blue eyes staring right through Elijah. "Eli hold your tongue damn it, we wouldn't even know about that train if it wasn't for G.O.D." Ezekiel chuckled, trying to break the tension. He was silenced by Paul who said, "Let the man speak." Paul's voice was cool and quiet. A thick tension settled across the room. Paul and Elijah had always been at it. It was now becoming apparent more and more that Elijah thought he was smarter and fitter to run the gang.

Elijah patted his short dirty blond hair and dropped his firm stance, "Hell Law, I'm only jagging you around just saying how I thought this was the last one. I'm nineteen now and not a young man anymore." This made Paul smile. He spoke, " I know I said this was it boys. It was a nice run and shit, altogether from the other jobs we got close to ten thousand a piece here. Yet I still feel twenty thousand a piece would be even better to retire on." "Boys, you know we ain't getting far without

Mr. God's help and shit boys, you know we ain't gonna get out of the damn State without that rich man's help." Law put his hands on his lap then stood up and walked around the table. "Hell, you thought we was free men out in the west. No, the wealthy are the only free men." "One more, boys and you will all be rich men serving none, living wherever you wish. " Je'sus spoke with his strong yet smooth accent, "Hey hermano, you can come to Mexico with me. Now that I have money I can raise horses." Moses spun a pistol on his finger forward before spinning it backward. He leaned back in his chair and spoke, "Why don't we just stay here? Shit, who's fucking wit us. Remember that Sheriff Bob and his gang of merry men?" "A bullet in his ass sent him flying off that horse and his men fleeing with their backsides in the cross-hairs of Eli's eagle eye getting fired upon." "Shit, only law in these parts is Paul Lawson and his gang so I hear. " Moses pulled out his chrome harmonica ready to play an eerie tune. His theme song.

Je'sus spoke, "Fuck, Moses how long you think that will last negro amigo? We're good but if they send Calvary down here we're finished." Je'sus missed his home even though it was a shanty town, while Moses thought of home as that farm in Georgia which disgusted him. Going back home meant working hard all his life only to die poor with no respect. "Send them, I got enough bullets." Moses replied, his eyes flashing. "Shit I'm a plant me a seed in some preacher's daughter soon enough I got dreams, but for now it's going good. What's the problem." He shrugged and put his brand new boots up on the table. Ezekiel added in, "Hell yeah!"

Elijah stood up. "Zeke, you're going to get yourself killed. We all are. What we do is wrong and I know I'm a burn in hell for it, I just want to have money and not die like my father struggling on this land barely eating."

Lawson spoke, "One more brothers, one more he told me and he will get us out of New Palestine. It kills me working for a fairy banker but shit he knows where the money is all ways and how to get it." "I'll find out tomorrow night, but take some money out boys, we're gonna see some whores before the last job. " Moses switched his tune to something a little more hip, whilst Elijah unveiled a banjo, and Zeke gave bass by blowing wind over a moonshine bottle. Moses dropped the vocals of a choir man, but his lyrics were not fit for a sailor's ears.

"Got money, got whiskey, got everything I need...... except some Pussy, some Pussssssssy!"

From outside the shabby deserted farm house all you could hear was hooting and hollering. The full moon's light bathed their foolish laughter and song. However, come morning the U.S. Marshals arrived at the Gainesville Train Station. The five Marshals walked through the crime scene led by William, who began explaining exactly what happened simply by looking at the bullet holes and tracks. "These youngsters are good little seasoned killers all ready," he said. "Bill, your son is out there talking to the passengers instead of in here learning something." Patrick spoke. William walked out to what was left of the train only to have Jeremiah jog towards him. "Marshall Evans, the passengers said a sniper on a ledge hit a man through a window while the train was moving." Jeremiah then added, "One woman describes this Lawson as well-mannered for an outlaw, but how they knew what was on the train is what I can't figure out."

William stopped him, "Kid, stay by my side and don't leave because it's about to get hairy." Just then a short balding man with spectacles walked over with a note in his hand. "Sir, telegram for Marshall Evans. " The note almost made William smile but he simply said, "Men mount up. " Teddy ran to his horse all the while shouting, "Wuuuuu, gonna get me sum finally." Dennis and Patrick simply smiled as usual eager to follow William to hell if need be.

In the small lawless town of Sancho was Hotel Sancho, which was a front for the bordello owned by Maggie O'Brien, where her girls welcomed the gang with hugs and kisses. She knew these boys were hotter than a pig in labor in the middle of summer as she said it, but also more importantly that they spent money. "Have whatever you want, fellas. Card games down stairs, women everywhere and whiskey and rum at the bar is on the house." Maggie said with a cool grin on her face. "Love you, Maggie!" was all the gang said except Law who just stared deeply in her eyes. "Naw, Paul before we start arguing you know you're my only man, but you keep saying you're gonna make me an honest woman. But what about you?" Maggie sighed, raising her eyebrow. "When you gonna give up the outlaw life?" Paul leaned in and spoke quietly to tell her that tomorrow would be his last job. After that, he would be. "Promise?" she replied. "Promise and enough money to take care of you for life." he replied. Law then picked her up and carried her up the steps in his arms.

About two hours had gone by since Eli had taken two women up to a room. One women held an opium pipe between her fingers. Inside the room, Eli drifted through a realm of ecstasy as this seemed to be the only time he was truly happy. Je'sus and Zeke sat at the bar drinking after their quick female escapades, cursing and laughing loudly while flashing their money. Moses was so drunk he was walking around in his underwear but still had his boots, hat, and revolvers on playing poker and grabbing up women. Finally, a man he was playing against had had enough and shouted, "God dammit! Put some clothes on and play the god-damn game! " "Or what?" Moses replied, stumbling to his chair and grabbing a woman to sit on his lap. "Or I'm a put some lead in your black ass, fucking knew not to play cards with a jig," the angry man muttered. The girl that was sitting on Moses lap knew it was time to move, the man did not know who Moses was. Two men that were with the card player stepped up, both of them larger in size by far. "Boy, get the fuck up from this table." The card player said. The card player leaned in. The glint in his beady brown eyes showed that he was going for his gun.

Moses leaned forward in the chair slurring from the booze with his eyes wide as he smiled. "You know, Lincoln freed the slaves but this here gun made 'em equal. " The man instantly went for his gun and exposed it over the table and fired, but lo Moses had dropped backwards towards the ground in the chair still, dodging the shot, and slid out a magnum and fired into the man's stomach before he hit the ground. The man grabbed his belly and looked down at the wound in shock. As soon as Moses hit the ground he instantly pulled his other revolver and with shots from both guns shot the two other men standing next to the card player. He dropped the two revolvers, stood up in a flash and pulled the other in his top front chest holster as he aimed back at the card player and let out a howl shaking his head frantically in agreement at his own skills, "Owwwwwweeeee! " The card player watched the blood pour out of his stomach before fixing Moses with a terrible frown. His face contorted angrily as he turned around reaching for a small blade lodged in his back and fell out of his chair to the floor dead. "Moses, you never leave any for me negro amigo!" Je'sus said merrily, over and removing the blade from the dead man's back. He wiped it off on the man's back as well before sticking it into a harness on his chest which held many more throwing knives.

Law entered on the top balcony, "Hand it's time to depart! " This shocked an onlooker who shouted, "Yawl are the Hand? "as he was flabbergasted that they were nothing but kids. Ezekiel approached drinking his beer, " Ahh yes we are." He then smashed the man over the head with the beer mug leaving him incapacitated. Elijah walked out of the room buckling his pants, "Yes, let us finish the story."

Under the night sky, the Marshal and his team sat getting ready to sleep in the wilderness for their day tomorrow as they would need their rest. "Jeremiah, what did your father do?" Marshal Evans asked, turning his gaze towards the young boy. Jeremiah replied that his father was a banker in New York. "Most all of my family is in finance sir," he said, looking into the fire. "Except you." William spoke. "Yes I suppose, it felt like something was pulling me" , Jeremiah replied. Teddy's sharp slanted blue eyes were fixed on J.J.

"Some prissy rich boy playing cowboy," Ted sneered. Marshal Evans fixed his eyes on Teddy quicker than his roar. "Shut your mouth fool, this man is smarter than you'll ever hope to be!" Marshal Evans continued to speak, "This ain't just hunting coyotes Ted, a man is different. I keep telling you, Jeremiah is schooled in criminal minds, he's studied this gang and he knows their character. That is what is needed for the future of this country, intelligent law men and not just some hot trigger moron wit shit for brains." Teddy's face dropped quickly and his face became as submissive as a puppy's. He mumbled,"Marshal I took down lots of men standing right next to you."

William seemed to just slide over across that flame and went face-to-face with Teddy as a ball of chew bulged in his cheek. "Yeah Ted, maybe too many. Now worry about these young devils. We're after them, not Jeremiah. Got it?" "Yeah I got it," Teddy replied. Dennis and Patrick said nothing and simply smirked at William as they were reminded about why he was nicknamed "The Old Wolf. " It had been two years since their last deployment and the reprimand that followed for the incident at Cherokee Field. William still didn't talk about it and stood by all his men until new orders were finally in.

The Marshal walked back and looked Jeremiah square in the eye, "You stand up and be a man son, don't be scared because that will get you killed out here. Or worse, make your heart black." Later, as the men went to sleep, Marshal's words spun in Jeremiah's head like the galaxy above as he laid there looking up at the night sky. His heart pounded quickly as he wondered if his father had been right.

Was he a fool for coming out here? Was he about to get himself killed? The night wind blew cold and made him shiver. Where was that fiery voice in his head that called him to the west, the one that passionately called him to deliver justice?

CHAPTER 3

Paul ran over the plan again while the gang rode through the countryside. "It's simple, really. This is Gainsville, the most heavily guarded town this side of Damascus but we have a way." He looked around with a grin on his face before continuing, "God's gonna have a man start a fire for us and that will be our queue to enter the First Gainsville Bank. In and out in five minutes tops looking to get fifty to sixty thousand in there brothers. No civilians as usual, all the men should be rushing for that fire meanwhile we're hitting safety deposit boxes 56, 27, 43, 13, and 10. Don't worry, I wrote them down." He pulled out a piece of paper proudly and finished, "Zeke got acid for the locks. No messing with the manager, just cover them. We get it and we're out easy."

The Hand settled inside an alleyway in Gainsville waiting for the signal, except Elijah who waited in the top of a storage barn with a perfect view of the bank about fifty yards away. In the lens of his scope he watched the boys post up eying the bank, except Moses who entered the local high-end tailor shop "Distinguished Gentlemen". Upon seeing Moses, the tailor walked up and quickly announced "Sir, I'm sorry but we cannot accommodate you in here." Moses dropped a spread of twenties on the front counter equaling two hundred dollars and replied, "Sure you can my good man, let me see your finest vest. " The tailor eyed his money for a second then proceeded to the back where a finer section waited. "Right this way, sir."

A bell rang as smoked filled the air over the post office. People went into a frenzy and ran to stare in disbelief at the blaze. Law smiled and walked towards the bank, he was nearing his destiny finally. All five fingers of The Hand including Elijah's all seeing eye fell together in the street and entered the bank in one casual motion. Zeke looked Moses up and down, "Had to get some new threads, huh. " "Can't be outlawin' looking dusty, that would just make you a thug." Moses said. A manager stood looking out the doorway with two female clerks behind him, "My Lord, the post office. What could have started this?" Upon noticing Law, the manager said "Sir, I'm gonna have to ask you to come back later. This is an emergency." Law stuck his revolver crested with the semblance of angels right underneath the man's chin. "Oh, I just need to make a quick withdrawal." The manager gasped. His glasses as well as his balding head caught the reflection of Paul Lawson. The outlaws all produced guns. Je'sus and Moses watched the two clerks while Law and Zeke hit the safety deposit boxes after the manager opened the gate. Zeke's acid burned right through the locks, a drop or two on each key hole then a smack and each one was opened. Forty three thousand dollars. Not as much as planned but still good for their last heist. The outlaws locked the manager and clerks up in the gate to safe before hearing a door shut. Four men stood in the doorway, bandannas over their faces as they held repeater rifles aimed at God's Hand. The one in the middle was a skinny man who was tall with sharp dark blue eyes and had high cheek bones. He pulled down his bandanna to show his boney face, "Who the fuck are you?"

Ezekiel replied up with chew in his bottom lip, "God's Hand, now get the fuck out of here." All the men in the room were standing face-to-face with no cover, gun-to-gun with the money in a bag in Paul's hand. Je'sus spoke up, "I know em! It's the "Douglas Boys", Charlie Douglas and his three brothers." Charlie smiled and spoke again, "Oh shit! The Hand! Damn boys we got celebrities in here." "Well sorry to tell you this, but this is our heist. We set the fire so hand the bag over. Bobby, grab it." The Douglas boys fully took aim, and Bobby, the youngest of the four, swiftly tried to grab the bag.

"Law, what do we do?!" Zeke yelled as the brothers took aim. Law replied, "Hand it over." He handed the bag to Bobby, who smiled like a well-fed crow and said, "Thanks fellas. We'll be leaving now." Bobby walked over to hand it to his other brother Ray. They were lined up perfectly symmetrical. A bullet crashed through the window and through both men's hearts. They dropped to the ground together in one final embrace. God's Hand immediately ran backwards blindly firing as the remaining Douglas Boys ducked incoming fire. All the men dove over the counter while in mid air as a shotgun shell from Zeke dropped Charlie's other brother Ben who was taking aim. Charlie dropped to the ground firing his rifle through the wooden counter rolling left to right all the while with no cover. He sat up to reload another cartridge in his rifle when Paul had him directly in his sights. He fired and picked up Charlie Douglas and delivered him through the Gainsville Bank window in one swift motion.

"Let's ride, men!" Paul shouted as he ran over and grabbed the bag off the floor. Moses ran through the door and into the streets which were still empty due to the chaos from the blaze. The others followed out the doorway until they saw a man in a long black trench with a shiny silver Marshal's badge. Looking down the street, Moses did not see him until it was too late and he was face-to-face with the Old Wolf, a ghost Elijah's perfect eye missed as well. William slapped a cuff on the three foot chain on Moses' right hand so that he dropped his revolver.

He spoke, "Think you're a man?" It was Marshal William Evans who spoke before raising his free right hand and clocking Moses square in the face. Moses was knocked to the ground and dropped his other pistol. The Marshal pulled him up by his bound hand and into a choke-hold as well as a shield and began firing at the outlaws. The young men ran inside as a bullet went through the glass of front door and by Law's head. The Hand flew for cover inside the bank as the other three marshals appeared from behind cover to fill the bank full of lead with rifles.

The firing was so close to the outlaws they couldn't even fire back at the risk of getting hit. Moses was stuck in the man's hold, helpless and unable to reach his firearms. William yelled, "Hold fire! " "You boys come out guns down hands up and I promise you won't get hung - just life in jail! " Je'sus eyes widened as he spoke, "These are Marshal's boys! We're fucked."

Moses grew in fury and back head-butted William and exclaimed, "Hell with that boys! FIRE! " God's Hand fired on everyone but William, pinning the marshal's men down for a second. William stumbled back with the chain extended. He looked up, saw a lamp post and threw the chain up over the post before pulling Moses up in the air and delivering a blow right to the young man's stomach before using his body for cover as he fired into the bank. Moses hung lifeless as the outlaws were pinned down, and the rest of the Marshals opened fire again. Moses shouted in pain and with spit flying kicked William in the face with his boot and spur. The Marshall, spitting blood mixed with chew, pulled the chain to break the wooden post sending Moses to the ground. Bullets fired from both sides between old William and young Moses, so close it felt like breezes in the wind to the men. Moses got on his feet and tugged the chain till it was fully extended and screamed, "Elijah! "

A bolt of lightning struck the chain separating it and the two. William immediately yelled, "cover! " The shots from Elijah kept Moses covered as he grabbed his revolvers while he ran to his horse. The marshals were pinned as the remaining Hand moved out firing and running for their horses. All the outlaws made it on horse and were headed out-of-town firing while Ezekiel lit a stick of dynamite with a match and tossed it in the direction of the Marshals. The blast had the men diving for cover as Zeke went to light another. When he turned, there right across from him was J.J. with his head down cowering in cover and a sparkling badge that read 'Marshal'.

Paul yelled, "Come on, Zeke." Ezekiel didn't listen. He hopped off his horse walked over and picked Jeremiah up by his shirt. "Son, you ain't built for this life. Looks like you're gonna find that out the hard way. " He slid a lit stick in Jeremiah's coat pocket and in a few seconds, an explosive bang sounded. Jeremiah slid out of Zeke's grip, leaving his coat behind as he ran the other way. As Jeremiah ran through an alley, he realized he almost forgot the dynamite in his pocket. He grabbed the stick of dynamite, tossed it, and dove for cover. An explosion rung out as a dust cloud behind Ezekiel rose up. He turned to face his brothers in crime and clinched his stomach oozing blood.

"No! " Elijah cried and fired everything he had at

the law men. Je'sus rode over, scooped the slow-moving Ezekiel and rode off all the while gunfire from both sides still blazed. They rode off as fast and as far as they could, while Eli pinned the Marshals down from afar before exiting quickly on his own horse as well. A few minutes later, William walked out of cover sensing the sniper was gone and spoke to a quivering Jeremiah, "Son, you made me proud. Don't worry, we're gonna get em. "

After miles of riding, Elijah stopped and dismounted. The gang did as well. Elijah walked over to Zeke who was still hugging Je'sus' back. He knew it before he even saw his sleeping face that his brother was dead. Elijah cried out in pain as he pulled his brother down to the ground in his arms. "What the fuck what was that, Paul? We were setup!" he shouted, cupping his face with his hands in anger. All the men turned to look at Law who replied, "I don't know. But he was my brother too." Eli pulled a pistol on Law, "My brother, my brother, and your god set us up."

Lawson got even closer to Eli, "I swear to you a man who has crossed my brother has crossed me, I will see to God personally." His face was grim and solemn as he spoke. "Right now though, we will take vengeance on these Marshals and show them why they call us God's Hand. And unto the man that kills this boy my entire share of this heist, brothers! " Elijah lowered his weapon as Paul bent down and kissed Zeke on the forehead. Zeke still gripped J.J.'s coat and inside that coat was his journal. Law grabbed it out and read the first page. It held an inscription from Jeremiah's mother, "To my beautiful son, Jeremiah Justice, may God be with you on your journey. " Law stood up and spoke, "My whole share to the man that kills JEREMIAH JUSTICE."

CHAPTER 4

For hours, the Marshals rode looking for those young men. It was now personal. William knew that those boys would run after the earlier encounter, and he had never lost a man he tracked. He received another telegraph while in Gainsville which told the location of the Hand's hideout. Jeremiah rode fast and close to William. By now, the rest of the men had accepted him. All but Teddy who glared at Jeremiah sharply every now and then. Dennis and Patrick, however, had both shaken Jeremiah's hand and congratulated him for taking one of God's Hand down. At this, William told the whole gang to focus. They had gotten caught off guard earlier, and their next target was the sniper. The Marshals were bringing law to the untamed land and they knew the land would sure fulfill it.

William stopped to give the horses a break at a pittstop and went down a trail to relieve himself at the service outhouse. Teddy crept over towards Jeremiah then spoke, "Didn't think you had it in you, college boy. Thought you was just gonna stand there with your tail between your legs." Ted smirked. "Don't get excited. You just stay low behind me." Pat stepped in and confronted Ted, "Ted, give him a break! " Ted turned, raised his eyebrows and shook his head while chuckling. "You love this kid now too?" William came out of the outhouse buckling his paints when a revolver with several pieces of cloth wrapped around it was pressed into his heart. "Caught you with your pants down, Marshal." Law's voice spoke soft and cold in the Marshal's ear.

William turned to Paul and spoke calmly, "Son, that boy is gonna kill you. Justice catches up with us all eventually. Even me." A pop went off, William grunted before going for his revolver. Another pop sounded. William dropped to his knees starring past Law's head to the heavens and smiled before rolling on his back. The Hand was split in half searching for the Marshal's Law and Moses. They were out numbered but laid a crushing blow to the law men. Law slid back into the woods to meet Moses. "Let me take out the rest Law." He said, loading up his gun. Law shook his head. "No, it's risky still and I want them to suffer. I will pick them off one by one. Let's head back."

Jeremiah thought he heard something. Why was William taking so long? He walked down the trail, "Marshal?" When he saw his mentor lying dead on the ground, Justice ran over to William who lay on his back panting. Looking up at Jeremiah, he smiled slowly and handed him his still clutched Eagle Revolver before fading into an eternal sleep. Jeremiah fell back on his heels and cried out. Dennis and Pat shot up and ran to Jeremiah. The men went searching, but couldn't see anyone anywhere in sight. Teddy simply stood there in shock of his leader dying, then knelt down and pulled a note out of Williams shirt pocket. Teddy said, "I got an address. We bury him then we move and kill all these little bastards. "

The marshals arrived at the bordello of Hotel Sancho by nightfall, they didn't speak at all. Jeremiah held Williams' Eagle Revolver on his hip now, his eyes were hot as fire and burning with anger and mourning. Teddy walked up and kicked the door open. The piano player halted and the whores and men stopped their laughing.

"My name is Marshal Teddy Johnson and I'm looking for a group of young outlaws calling themselves The Hand." " His dark eyes searched the room. "Now it's been told to me that these evil bastards frequent this here establishment. " Maggie stepped up, "Marshal, I can assure you for good sir their is no one here by that descrip......" Teddy pointed his finger in Maggie's face and cut her off. "I haven't even given you a description yet honey, now where are they? " You could see that the rest of the Marshals looked uncomfortable by the way Teddy treated Maggie. He snatched her by her long blonde hair, "I'm not gonna ask you again whore." Dennis stepped forward with his hand raised and spoke, "Ted, that's enough." "Alright... you're right, Dennis. I don't wanna hurt this pretty little thing. Hell, that would be a crime but I WILL HURT THIS LITTLE CHINA DOLL HERE, NOW TALK! " Ted grabbed Lin Su by her long silky black hair and all the girls were screaming by this time as the male patrons cowered in silence. Ted tossed Lin Su back so hard she flew across the room as if she were made of paper. Ted lunged at Lin Su to hurt her. "TALK!" Jeremiah had seen enough. In a flash, he stood between Ted and Lin Su and shoved the man so hard he fell on his back. "That's enough!" Ted was in shock and embarrassed as he sat on his bottom now. He got up and in one straight line was heading for J.J. His face contorted with anger, he snarled, "Boy, have you gone out of your mind? " J.J. stood face-to-face with Ted. Although he was afraid of standing up to Ted, he spoke with a steady voice. "No, you're the one who's crazy. Law men don't hurt the innocent." The corner of Ted's mouth curled up in the hint of a smile, "Son, ain't no one innocent especially out here. " Ted tried to go around J.J. to grab Lin Su who was now crouching in a corner shaking, but as soon as he tried J.J. threw a devastating right hook punch that made everyone from the other Marshals to Zeus and the other Gods of Mount Olympus drop their jaws in disbelief. Ted was finally off his chain and attacked

Jeremiah as a wolf pouncing on a lamb. J.J. fought back the best he could, but in an instant was a bloody mess on the floor. Ted had his boot on the side of the young man's face when Maggie stepped in. She stared at Teddy blankly before saying, "They're in an old barn on the road between Maysville and Old Elnero." Ted stepped back and smirked softly. "Now see, that wasn't so hard." He turned and took his rage away from Jeremiah. "Kid, you can stay here with the whores since you love them so much. Told you this life ain't for you. Come on boys. " The other Marshals turned to leave with a sad grim look on their faces before taking one last look at the young man who was coughing up blood in Maggie's arms. They walked out the door without a word.

Jeremiah awoke to the sounds of birds chirping and Lin Su's pretty smile. She looked radiant even with a bruise on her forehead, as she wiped his face with a damp cloth. Maggie spoke from a chair in the corner of the room cracking her knuckles, "That was a brave thing what you did, not most men would have done that and I know men." J.J. tried to sit up but could barely do so speaking, "More like a crazy thing. I was a fool thinking I could come out here and make a difference in the world." "You're not stupid and you're not a kid. What I saw last night was a man amongst boys with badges," Maggie said. Jeremiah frowned, "Look what it got me, the living tar kicked out of my guts. I'm a fool...I don't know what I was thinking." Maggie leaned forward, her brilliant eyes shining. "So, what were you thinking?" she asked, tilting her head. Jeremiah paused deeply in thought before replying,"I don't know. Something inside made... I can't explain. But look what my 'brave thinking' got me." He then rolled on his side away from the women in disgust and shame. Lin and Maggie looked at each other in sadness. Maggie stood up and walked over to J.J. and stroked his short black hair. "I've done a lot of wrong in this life, taken wives' husbands in my bed and not for just the money but more for sport." She sighed and sat on his bed, looking into the far distance. "It's time I did something right. This old life is over for me and for you as well. It's time we make a new life for ourselves. Your soul is broke and hopeless, just like this wall I built up around my heart." She stood up now, determined. "I know an old Engine that can fix you and help you find your true path. If you're interested, I'm staring a new life out east to be a better person and it will start with fixing you. If you want to join me, we'll get the horses ready and be on our way."

Maggie and J.J. rode along an old dusty trail into Indian territory. J.J. had black and blue marks across his face as he was aching from every step the horse took. They rode for hours, sharing their childhood stories with each other so that by the time they reached their destination at the top of a secluded cliff, they were good friends. Maggie turned and swiftly hopped off her horse. J.J. raised his eyebrow and suppressed a grin. She did not ride like a lady to say the least. Maggie approached an old shack with spirit catchers, wind chimes, and beads hung about everywhere. An old wooden door opened and a man who looked to be in his fifties came out in Cherokee dress with his hair in two braids . His wrinkled face told of great wisdom from past ages in his mind. J.J. thought this man's ways are of a mystic people whom the white man came here and crushed, all because his ways were different. The old Indian smiled warmly. "Maggie!" He walked over to her. "Good to see you again, I have some new smoke for you." Maggie exclaimed, "Somebody, oh I missed you." She turned to introduce the two. "Somebody, this is Jeremiah. Jeremiah, this is Somebody." Jeremiah looked puzzled and said, "Somebody?" The old man replied, "Yes well, it is "He Who Tells Us Who We Really Are". My People call me this because they say I am always telling them to have pride and to keep their heads up and remember who they are." He winked. "I prefer the name Somebody though." J.J. sat there on his horse silent in disbelief.

Somebody bid them to all come in and have tea, and that evening Maggie went in the back room alone with Somebody and spoke alone with him before coming out to bid J.J. good bye. "Jeremiah, this will probably be the last time we speak." She looked at him with a resolved expression. "Somebody will give you your new path...I told him all about you." Maggie looked at him with a watery eyes then came closer slowly and kissed him on his lips. Jeremiah whispered, "Maggie?" She then turned and left the room quickly. Somebody entered the room, "Maggie has told me much about your heart and how its drum beats. Do you know what your drum beats for?" Jeremiah surveyed the old man skeptically before saying quietly, "No." "It beats for Justice no?" Somebody said with a smile. Somebody was concocting a strange brew in his kettle on the fire and it was full of all types of strange ingredients he pulled from his shelves and smelled of burning dung. He poured some in a cup and walked outside and beckoned Jeremiah to follow. They walked to the edge of the cliff where a stone bed lay. Somebody pointed to the slab for JJ to sit on and gave him the cup to drink. He took one sip and almost spit it out. "That's horrible!" Jeremiah said. "Drink it, you must so we can see who you really are." Somebody said. Jeremiah downed the entire cup then gagged. "Aghh, That tastes like shit." "Coyote shit to be exact." said Somebody. Jeremiah looked at him with the shock of a teenage girl finding out she was pregnant. "Jeremiah, there is so much evil in men's hearts, these days more than old, and in these parts more than others. Few men wish to do right, and even fewer will not stand by quietly while wrong is being done." Somebody turned to look at the sky before fixing his eyes on the young boy. "Jeremiah, why did you come here?" Jeremiah answered, "Because a voice told me to." Somebody replied, "What did it say?" Jeremiah answered, "I need you." Somebody closed his eyes and stopped pacing and said, "It is time, you are the one." Jeremiah looked up at the stars in the night sky as they began to move and dance until they became an eagle and that eagle soared high in the heavens and than came down in the physical and landed on a perch next to Jeremiah. "Hey! Somebody let out aloud cry and began chanting and then spoke. "You are the one Jeremiah, the one the Earth has called out to give JUSTICE to this land."

Jeremiah looked away. He staggered out of shock at the sight."I must be dreaming." "Or are you waking up?" Somebody asked. He pulled out a large blade and approached the quivering young man, "Jeremiah look deep in your heart and tell me what you want most of all in this life?" Jeremiah paused looked the old Native right in the eyes and replied,

"To protect the weak and innocent." "Stick out your hand." said the Earth's Priest. Just then the eagle landed on Jeremiah's forearm and let out a mighty screech. J.J. flinched from the talons of the eagle gripping his forearm. The eagle got eye-to-eye with Jeremiah who dared not make the slightest of moves for fear of getting his eyes pecked out. Somebody grabbed Jeremiah's hand and cut it deep as the blood dripped down into the dust of the Earth. The mighty eagle then turned around and stuck its neck out willingly. Somebody looked at Jeremiah's uncertain eyes and said, "You are the one whom the Earth has chosen as it's protector, from now on your name is simply Justice." He then cut the eagle's neck and its blood poured out and into Jeremiah's open wound. The old Indian held the bird and Justice's arm as their blood mixed. Justice laid down on the slab and watched the stars as Somebody chanted the same tomes his grandmother used to. The Universe spun, the coyotes howled, the mountains and the sky melted one into another and Jeremiah slept to be awoken in the morning as "Justice". But what that meant he still did not fully understand.

Justice awoke to the rooster's call. He stared at the cracked mud ceiling then jumped out of bed, not sure of where he was. "Tea." Somebody spoke out from within a doorway. "Yes, thank you." Justice replied. Somebody didn't say anything about last night. He just stared at Justice and smiled. He spoke up after some time. "What do you plan on doing?" Justice replied, "I guess going home, back to my father in shame. Tell him I was wrong and he was right." "And what do you feel like doing Justice?" His pale face and dark brown eyes looked off at the wall as if a window to the supernatural world was at that spot. "Ride after all them boys and if they all don't come quietly, kill em." One of Somebody's eyebrows rose as he spoke, "You would still give them the option to keep their life even though they killed your teacher?" Justice turned in disbelief of himself and spoke softly, "Yes I would." Somebody nodded at his answer and seemed to understand. He gently said, "Let's eat a big breakfast. You'll need it before your journey." The two men ate delicious fry bread the size of Justice's head and then Justice packed his things and mounted his horse.

Before he left, he started to say "Somebody, about last night..." Before he had a chance to finish his sentence, Somebody spoke up, "Justice, an old friend from the land of the rising Sun left this here. I'm giving it to you." It was an old leather satchel. Justice took it from Somebody and felt the worn leather against his smooth hands. Somebody had a hint of a smile when he said, "I think you need it more than I do." When Justice took a look inside, he turned his face back up at Somebody with his mouth open in awe. "Take care, Justice and remember our paths are laid out for us by the Great Creator before we are even born. Fear not." Somebody walked off into his house singing an old Negro hymn. "Down on the river Jordan......." His deep voice faded off as his back became smaller and smaller. When he finally disappeared from sight, Justice rode down the hill. Somebody peeked at him through the crack of his door with a slight smile on his face.

CHAPTER 5

A dirt road is the only thing separating the wilderness from civilization. The Sun spread its reach through the tall trees scattered across the wilderness as Justice came to a fork in the road. He was not sure if he should head back to the train station or continue on with his mission. He closed his eyes and wiped his brow. He listened to his heart beat and waited. Something in his instincts told him to continue. He took the furthermost path from the station on the road less traveled which led him deeper in the brush to a pool where he climbed off his horse to help it get a drink and rest. "Easy, Liberty. Rest up." Jeremiah kneels down to get a drink in his hands and then feels heat on him. He looks up to see a figure staring at him from across the pond. "Amigo!" Je'sus said, a devilish smiling appearing on his face. His eyes glinted with triumph and malice. "I've been looking for you everywhere."

Je'sus peered across the small water hole smiling at Justice. Jeremiah was frozen jaw aghast, dead to rights he knew the Mexican had him. He could see the pistol in his hand. Je'sus spoke, "I was going to just leave my gang and this lifestyle and go home. That's what my heart said, but then here you are." He stepped forward. "Kid, you killed my friend and for that I'm going to kill you. But, I'll give you a sporting chance because a man should have a chance in this life and there are too many cowards in this country." Je'sus cracked his shoulders. "If you can make it away from me on your horse, you are free to go on my honor." A feeling came over Jeremiah and it was so strong that it felt foolish. He closed his mouth, stood tall and shouted, "Je'sus Alvarez, you are under arrest for the crimes of murder and robbery. Come quietly or face your fate." Je'sus was not amused, "You have ten seconds. Diez, nueve, ocho!" Justice leapt on his horse and bolted forward in a rush.

Down the road, Liberty ran fast as she could. She

sensed Jeremiah's fear. But fear makes one think fast. Justice pulled his pistol. Behind him, he could hear the mad man screaming, yelling and whistling as if this was a game. Justice turned and fired the first shot but the bullet went right over the horses head and past an empty saddle. Je'sus rode all the way on the side of the horse using it for cover. He swiftly ran close to the ground before poking his head up and firing at Justice. Jeremiah heard the bullet whiz by. He knew he could not get a clear shot as the Mexican Indian was a pro-rider who had been a cattle thief since twelve. Just then, he looked over to his right and saw Je'sus right next to him. He had caught up. "You lose amigo!" Je'sus jumped up completely standing on his horse's back. Showing off his talents, Justice took aim but Je'sus turned and fired quickly as he was used to shooting on horseback. The bullet grazed Justice in the shoulder and he almost fell off his horse but held on for dear life. The Mexican smiled the devil's smile and jumped down on his horse to slow up to Jeremiah.

"Amigo, this is the end. Don't cry! Face death like a man, Areeba!" Justice knew he was out of his element. He still got sick from heavy riding, his stomach was in his heart, and his heart was in his throat. He had to make a move so he leaned up and forward and gripped Liberty's harness tight then veered off into the thick forest off the path. Liberty jumped right in the dense bush leaping over logs and stones making her own path. Je'sus was not amused. "You can't run from me gringo!" He yelled as he followed Justice in.

Here in the wilderness, his horse was not as used to the terrain so Justice got some distance on him. Just enough to time to think, Jeremiah thought. What could he do? If he slowed down to try to get into a gun battle with this guy, he'd be done. He knew Je'sus had been playing with him the whole time and now it was the final hand. His clock was almost up, his star was burning out. "Wait!" He had an idea. He veered hard back towards the road. Je'sus was pissed, he had had enough. He charged and kicked his horse harder and harder to follow. Justice had reached the dirt road again and Liberty leaped on to it. He knew he had only one chance. He reached in his shirt pocket and grabbed a match out and struck it off his cheek. Reaching in the satchel Somebody had given him at the same time he pulled out a single long stick of dynamite and ignited it. The timing had to be perfect as Je'sus came flying up out of the brush as if Satan himself was riding the White Horse out of hell's fiery pit. Je'sus whipped his horse faster and faster and closer and closer to Justice before aiming his pistol directly at his target's back. Justice extended his arm and dropped the stick. Je'sus was puzzled. What did Justice drop? As he got closer and closer, he peered down and made out the spark at the end of its line. And Je'sus Alvarez spoke his last word, "Calbrone".

The explosion of dirt and smoke made Je'sus' horse stop in fear and rear back on its two front legs flinging the rider off. Je'sus flew off flying through the air, through the smoke with no control, and face first into the hard ground below. Justice rode over to his lifeless body very slowly gun out. There was a body and a hat but only remnants of a face. He took the machete off Je'sus' back then got back up on Liberty before petting her side to calm her. He could feel her shock. The explosion had shaken her as well.

With a few pats he calmed her and they both turned at the same time and rode down the path together as one.

Maggie was back at the brothel now. She packed her last suitcase then smiled at Lin Su, "Almost out of this shit hole Lin." "Back east men know how to treat a lady, they still dogs but dogs that knows how to treat a lady." Lin Su smiled then spoke, "I'm afraid our past will follow us." "The past is the past and if you don't like the fact that I was a whore hands off the ass!" Maggie said proudly. This made Lin Su giggle. "Besides Lin we got enough money we don't need no man honey, gonna open me a nice little women's shoe store". "Have you thought of a name?" Lin Su asked. " All I need is shoes" Maggie replied, zipping up her suitcase. Lin Su quietly smiled in agreement.

The two had been sharing their thoughts on the recent chaotic events all morning as they were closing up shop. Maggie always trusted her gut and never got involved with anyone else's business. However, this time she did. Women had been slapped before in her establishment and from time-to-time she had to pull out her shotgun from behind the bar counter. But it was always just business, except this time she had helped an enemy of Paul Lawson. She could feel her unprecedented good deed coming back to haunt her. Regardless, Jeremiah was the first real gentleman she had seen since, well, a very long time. She hoped maybe Somebody had just given him a good pep talk then sent him on his way back home. Like he did for her when she felt like killing herself from time-to-time. But something was different, something was in the air and coming for her. The end of the road was near. She felt it. Maggie paid off all the girls in the bordello and said her goodbyes. Some women in her position hopped a train and went back home while some went to another whorehouse the next county over. What was waiting in store for them? It was just her and Lin Su now and they were on a train to Boston in the morning with over $10,000 – or so they hoped.

The Marshals crept around the sides of God's Hand's hideout, Patrick at the back door and Dennis at the side window. After a split-second, Teddy kicked in the door. None of them kids was getting taken in alive. Patrick kicked in the back door as well while Dennis aimed through the window. But the place was empty with just Ezekiel's homemade moon shine sitting on the table. Teddy poured a shot then spoke, "The goddamn little fuckers ain't here. We'll wait around a while for them then backtrack up stream. They have to be close by." "Hey Teddy, who made you boss?" Patrick asked, his eyes looking over Teddy with contempt. "I don't recall voting you in." "Easy Pat, I just wanna get these little bastards." Patrick shook his head before saying, "Well you been barking a lot of orders lately, and that shit you pulled back there at that whorehouse ain't gonna fly!" Dennis nodded silently. "It got us the information we needed, didn't it!" Teddy yelled. Teddy and Patrick got face to face. "Easy!" Dennis said, trying to break up the tension. "Fuck Pat, these bastards killed Bill. Now don't you want to get them for that?" Teddy asked. Patrick sighed then replied, "Yes." "Well then, let's do what it takes to get the job done, and if some whores gotta get smacked and a couple heads get cracked so be it."

Patrick shrugged his shoulders and let out a sigh

of surrender. Under Teddy's orders the men ducked off about 100 yards from the shack and waited to see if the gang returned. But the three fingers that was left of God's Hand rode down the road together in the next county over searching for Justice and Je'sus, who had not returned at the meeting spot as planned yesterday. They were hungry for revenge. A city slicker kid killing a member of the gang was an abomination, it was unacceptable. But deep down they all knew the end had been coming to them for a while. They had been blazing a path of death and destruction across the state for two years now. All of them knew it was time for a change except Moses who accepted the outlaw life as the only life for him.

"When I find this pussy, I'm a cut him up real slow, carve the hand symbol on his chest and let him bake in the sun a couple days staked down." He said quietly. "We got to find him first." Law replied. He was just about to say something else when he saw an image on the road which made his jaw drop. Moses cried, "No!" Elijah whipped his horse and galloped up to the scene and what was left of the gang followed. "Je'sus!" Moses shouted. His eyes were wide in shock.

The gang was shocked in silence as it turned out that now two members of God's Hand had been killed. God's Hand that killed the McCormick boys, God's Hand that robbed the First Bank of America, God's Hand.... the gang that laughed at lawmen and blew kisses at Death. Je'sus was out looking solo for a long time and didn't meet back up with the gang. Law thought he ran back home but here his friend lay lifeless. This was devastating. Eli exploded, "Fuck, fuck this is it. I'm killing these little fuckers myself!" "Wait we'll kill them together." Moses said. chimed in "No, I'm done, done with all this, done with God's hand!"

Moses shook his head then spoke, "No Eli, we're a family. We're all we got out here." Eli looked Moses square in the eye and replied, "This ain't no family Moses." He then looked at Law with utter hatred and turned his horse and sped off. Moses screamed, "Eli, Elijah!" "Let him go. We'll bury our brother then rebuild the Hand." Law said.

CHAPTER 6

J ustice and Liberty rode down the dusty road. They were exhausted from the sun's rays. Justice hadn't even had time to reflect on the events of the morning, had he really been transformed into something else? He had killed two people - in self defense but none the less two people and it felt natural. His mind also kept replaying the eagle he saw from his vision at Somebody's house. Was it all real and did he have power to take another man's essence?

"Hey now!" An old man stopped him on the road. His face was dark as coal but shone like a diamond in the Sun under his straw hat. He held wheat in his mouth and a plow in his hand. "You looking parched young man, you ain't even see me here did ya!" "No sir supposed I didn't. Got a lot on my mind." Justice said. "Well, come on in and have yourself a drink a lemonade. The name is Steve. Friends call me Black Steve." He said.

Justice descended his horse and the two walked down the path to Steve's house. It lay at the bottom of a small hill with acres of wheat behind it as far as the eye could see. Justice tied Liberty next to a waterhole and went inside. The lemonade was like water being thrown on a house that blaze with fires from Lucifer's mouth. Justice leaned back in the chair and let out a sigh of relief. He hadn't stopped all day now that and now that he thought about it he hadn't eaten either. Black Steve must have heard his thoughts, "You hungry? I got some breakfast and some sweet potato pie left over." "Yes Sir, please." "You look like a nice young man. What's troubling you?" Black Steve asked. As Justice ate he felt obliged to tell Steve all that had happened. Also, Steve just had a certain wisdom to him to which made you want to hear his words to find guidance for your path. Just as Justice was finishing his tale, Steve chimed in at the end. "Yea, The Hand ain't no joke them boys worse then the clan. Best you clear out fast son." Justice looked away with spite in his heart. "Why can't you leave?" Steve asked.

Justice thought about it for a minute then told him the other half. He told him about the trip to Somebody's house and the spirit dream before asking Steve if he was crazy. asked, ""Hell naw!" Steve said. "My wife was full blood Cherokee. God rest her soul and you best believe!" Black Steve stared back at him incredulously. "No, no you have a destiny young man. Some people miss their destiny, but with others, well, destiny grabs hold of them and won't let go no matter what." Steve looked into Justice's eyes. "This is your destiny, son. This is your time. I seen it first time I looked at you." Steve said. He added, "You're the one who is gonna rid this land of evil. But you gotta believe in yourself. Look at your self in that mirror there son and tell me what you see." Jeremiah looked in the mirror. A young and boyish face stared back at him, eyes wide. Yet, a new sort of wisdom lay over his features. His gaze grew steady. He replied, "I see Justice." The reflection of Justice rugged, strong, pure rippled before shattering into pieces of glass to the ground. "Get down!"

Justice screamed as he dove for the kitchen floor.

In a grassy knoll with a large shrub right above his head Elijah Bordeaux, older brother of recently deceased Ezekiel Bordeaux, reloaded his bolt action rifle then spoke to himself, "A fucking mirror." The shot seemed to silence all manor of life in the area, the birds in the air, the crickets in the field. Even the ants on the ground knew the ugly truth that a man was about to die. Black Steve whispered to Justice, "The Hand?" "Yea." Eli yelled down at the house, "Justice you killed my brother!" Black Steve chimed in, puzzled and intrigued, "Justice?" Justice replied, "Jeremiah Justice at your service Sir." He tipped his hat but stayed lower than a caterpillar to the ground. Everyone knew of Elijah's rifle abilities in the State. But what Justice did not know was who else was all there lusting for his blood at the moment. Better ask, he thought. "Yea I did! What can I say, the man stuck a stick of lit dynamite in my pocket!" Black Steve looked at Justice in disbelief. Justice continued, "So what, you needed to bring the whole gang with you to take out one guy?" Eli almost smiled, "No Justice it's just me just me and you. "Justice was almost relieved he wasn't at a complete disadvantage. Liberty was tied up (a mistake he would never make again) and if he even stepped outside that door he was a goner. Steve spoke aloud to himself shaking his head, "If only my old eyes weren't so bad I'd pick this little fucker off. Think you can do it Justice?" Justice thought for a minute then spoke, "I ain't got no rifle Steve." Steve replied, "I got something better, Betsy." Steve's eyes looked up towards the mantle that held a bolt action cartridge rifle.

Justice got up and ran from the kitchen to the den and grabbed the rifle in one motion but as he crossed the living room window a shot rang out and a bullet nearly struck him. "I won't miss again Justice!" Eli said as he reloaded his bolt action rifle. "No you won't." Justice replied in a whisper as he crouched in a corner beside the fireplace. "Well?" shouted Steve. They looked at each other. "Well what?" Justice replied. "Shoot the motherfucker!" Black Steve hissed. Justice frowned at the old man, then ran things through in his head. He had a rifle now, but if he stuck his head up in any window in that small shack of a house he would be done for sure. Steve exclaimed in a low tone, "Justice, I got it. I got myself my own underground railroad under the house. Around the corner yonder there's a hatch that will lead you to a small tunnel underground."

Justice put the rifle strap over his head and crawled on his stomach with Betsy on his back to Steve's bedroom. In the room lay an old Indian blanket on the floor. Justice moved it to the side and underneath lay a trap door that he opened and crawled into. Underneath the house ran a tunnel about 4ft high, it was pitch black and murky. A lantern was hung at the entrance, Justice took a match, lit the lantern and began crawling. About one hundred yards off was the barn and the end of the tunnel. Justice arose out of the trap door very slowly and quietly. His every step carefully considered, he considered all the reports on Elijah Bordeaux. Elijah's reputation for hitting men right between the eyes a hundred yards off. His lust for opium and the whores that brought the pipe. His love of his only family, his orphaned brother whom Justice had killed.

Justice inched out just over a bundle of hay and

took aim through the barn entrance and up upon the hill where Eli was firing from. He scanned the hilltop but saw nothing. He took aim at Steve's house all around but saw nothing. He viewed in all directions he could for an hour, but saw nothing except crows and rabbits. His knees ached and the sweat dripped and burnt his eyes. He wiped his forehead and took down his rifle, he looked at the stairs and then headed for them. Up very, very slowly and quietly until he was upstairs. The view from the upper level barn opening was wider and more open so his vision was clearer. Now just where did Eli go? He setup over another hay bundle, he was not gonna be hunted like some scared prey. He emptied his mind trying to fill where Eli was, and then he felt someone was watching him. He took his eye out from the scope. Justice slowly turned to his left to see Elijah with both hands on his rifle aimed out the same barn window, but his face was looking directly at him. The two young men said nothing, they just stared at each other for what seemed like a lifetime.

In those few seconds that went on like eons, Justice knew one wrong move would be the end of him. Taking aim with his rifle in hand was a fifty fifty and that was way too low of a percentage when life and death are concerned. Was he faster than Eli on the draw with a hand gun? Fifty fifty once again, but then he had it. A diversion is what he needed. Justice in one swift motion threw his rifle at Eli, and in one motion Eli aimed. But the rifle was bout to crack Eli right in the face, so Elijah dropped his rifle and caught Betsy in-mid air before it cracked him. As Eli took focus from the rifle he could see Justice coming at him full speed screaming like a mad man wielding Je'sus' machete pulled from his back sheath. There was no time to pull his pistol, he did the only thing he could, he blocked the strike with the rifle. The top edge of the blade almost reached Eli's face, he pushed back for life. Was this the same punk tender-foot that killed his brother? Was he to end Elijah's life as well? Then from the pits of Elijah's stomach came Satan himself. This was the man who killed his baby brother. He pushed back with a yell then went for his bowie knife to plunge it into Justice's heart. Justice flew back unscathed ready to strike again as a panther for the kill. The two were in arms reach, blades out fighting as the ancients did blade-to-blade and man-to-man. A twirl of the machete by Justice followed by a quick side slash at Elijah's stomach. Justice dodged Eli's attack to catch him off-guard, but Eli returned the favor with a slash at Justice's face. Justice parried swiftly and dodged the attack by inches.

The two circled each other atop the old dusty barn, funny how smells of mildew and animal dung become non-existent when one's life is at jeopardy. "You killed my brother Jeremiah," said Elijah. "Well he was tryna kill me first." Jeremiah replied. Eli grew quiet, only hatred and vengeance boiling in his heart now. He and his brother were orphaned and had no one else but each other before God's Hand. Now everything was all gone, all that love would never return. But he would end this man's life in revenge. Elijah lunged at Justice with everything he had so that their blades met metal-to-metal. But Elijah was possessed with anger. Spit and foam flew from his mouth as he lunged. Justice fell to one knee. Just as he fell to the floor, he heard his father's words echoing in his mind, "You're going to get yourself killed! "

Water filled his eyes then Justice felt something rushing through him. Years of practicing knife-wielding and knife-throwing all at his finger tips had taught him some special tricks. He knew an and simple easy maneuver that might just save his life. Justice spun away to the side as all of Eli's momentum took him forward and Justice struck at his back leg all in the same motion. Eli let out a gasp and almost a whimper before grabbing his back thigh. Eli limped for a second then stood straight up ready to strike. Justice said nothing, no expression on his face. He just starred back at Elijah. Eyes red and face contorted in anger, Elijah furiously let out a blood-curdling scream as he charged Justice again. This time, a quick parry of Justice's blade took him to the ground and the impact of the his fall made Justice's machete fly out of his hand. Eli was on top of him now with both hands looking to plunge the six inch blade in Justice's throat. With one hand Justice tried to hold him off while reaching for his machete but it was out of reach.

The bladed inched closer and closer, Justice

needed to think fast again. He looked in Elijah's eyes they were as a wild beasts, then it hit him like lightning. An old skill he used before earlier that day. Justice abandoned his efforts for his blade and took both hands and pushed Eli's blade back just enough to make room. He than reached in his shirt pocket and pulled out a match and struck it off his cheek. Eli, puzzled, almost stopped trying to kill him for a second. With the lit match Justice pulled it down to his waist as he lifted up his backside and lit a stick of dynamite on his waist. He then dropped the match, removed the stick and placed it into Eli's coat pocket. Eli looked at Justice and was unable to hide a slight smile, the same expression that his dearly deceased brother often wore. Elijah flew off of Justice, dropped his knife and removed the lit stick of dynamite to the floor. It fell in between both of them. Neither even thought about firing a shot at each other, Eli grabbed his beloved rifle and headed for the barn window. Justice still on the ground pulled in Betsy with one arm and his machete with the other and ran in the opposite direction.

Justice sheathed his machete in a flash and threw

his rifle around his neck. The direction he was headed in had no exit, just a wall. There were seconds left on that dynamite wick. No time, Justice thought. He would have to make an exit. There. that spot seemed weak as it was mostly loose and decaying wooden boards. He crashed through it and was in mid-air heading face-first for the ground as was Elijah on the opposite side. Both hit the ground and rolled at the same time before getting up and continuing their battle through the wheat fields. The explosion shook the heavens and blew a hole in the barn roof. Steve exited his front door in awe. Then he was pissed. "My barn, you little mother fuckers, my barn!" he shouted. But no one replied to his exclamations and rants.

Deep in the wheat fields, Justice lay on the ground not moving and too scared to move an inch. He knew moving and shaking the wheat too much would give away his position. Eli could be one hundred yards away or just ten. This day was getting worse and worse, but he was in the fire now. Justice would not allow negative thoughts of retreat or self-pity to enter his mind. This was life and death in all its ugly beauty, and deep down he knew this chaos would always be a part of him. The clouds danced over Justice's head while he tried to think of something, but he just drew a blank. Nothing materialized in front of him. He only saw a beautiful sky, wheat and a scarecrow. Justice's eyes filled with tears and he gasped. The time was now. He stuck his thumb and middle finger in his mouth and let out a loud whistle. Liberty shrugged and pulled trying with all her might to break free of the post she was tied to. Steve seeing the steed's desire to be free ran over as fast as his old legs would take him and grabbed an axe next to a wood pile to set her free. Liberty darted off, fleeing quickly to her brother's call. Faster and faster, she got closer and closer until she was at the edge of the field. A figure moved quickly then out flung Justice's long coat flowing in the wind so that with one leap the rider was on the horse.

Elijah smirked before he pulled the trigger exposing himself about thirty yards away in the same field. The bullet hit its target right on and the body hit the ground as Liberty kept galloping onward. Eli took his time walking over. Finally, he had avenged his brother. Now it was over, not the way he wanted it to end but over nonetheless. He got closer and closer to Justice's body smiling with content at his abilities. He froze when he approached the body and saw the smiling painted face of a scarecrow beaming back at him. Justice emerged, his face and body lined with brush burns and bruises from hitting the ground. While hanging on the side of Liberty, he had pulled the scarecrow and his attire off at just the right time to dodge the bullet. Elijah had no time to react as Jeremiah let out a grizzly bear yell and then a machete's blade pierced its self directly through Elijah's chest. He let out a horrendous scream and fell to his knees before turning his head to face Justice. Blood spouting and coughing Elijah spoke, "Smart Justice. Maybe smarter than the Law." Their eyes met and suddenly there was an intimacy akin to that of brothers and family. A tear rolled down Elijah's face. A grim look of anguish came across Justice's features as he quickly pulled the blade out of the last Bordeaux brother and Elijah fell on his back looking up at the heavens. His eyes empty, he gave up the ghost, and was no more. Justice stood over him for a few minutes thinking how this long played-out chess match was over in just one swift move. Eli's eyes were wide open staring back at him so Justice removed his glasses, put them in his shirt pocket, and closed his eyes so the "All Seeing Eye" could finally get some rest.

CHAPTER 7

Teddy, Patrick, and Dennis rode down the the dusty trail towards the local telegraph station. Dennis and Patrick were deathly quiet, but Teddy could sense what was on their minds. "Don't worry boys, they're close. These punks ain't leaving the state... they think they run it but they're gonna find out who is in charge very soon," he said as he dismounted his horse and walked into the telegraph station. Dennis looked over to Patrick as if waiting for him to say something. They glared at each other in a silent argument. Finally, Patrick spoke after a few seconds passed. "Fuck Dennis, what you want me to do?" "What do I want you to do is back me up when I put this psycho in his place!"He cast a suspicious glance towards the telegraph station before leaning in and speaking softly, "Pat. Pat, remember the Apache Canyon Incident? This asshole. One psycho we let loose and keep covering for and now all our souls are damned." Teddy then exited the telegraph station with a big grin on his face and shouted, "Men, we got these little bastards mount up!"

Moses rode down the road following Elijah's trail until they spotted a moving figure in the distance on a hill top. The two galloped up to the top of the hill before dismounting and walking over. Both Moses and Law stared at the old black man who was finishing filling in the hole. They were in shock at the sight of a makeshift wooden cross above and Elijah's rifle wrapped around it. Their mouths fell open. Moses felt sick to his stomach while Law felt his eyes water. Not so much for their fallen comrade, but more because they knew their end was soon to come and to pass for it seemed that this turn of events was divinely orchestrated. Law looked at the old man. No, it was not him who had done this. He turned and looked at the hole in the barn roof then turned and thought in silence. Steve stood up, dusted the dirt off his trousers and answered the question before he could even ask it. "You know who it was. He's gone now. Fuckers blew a hole in my barn though." He shook his head and glanced towards the grave. "Your friend deserved a christian burial nonetheless."

"And for that old coon, I won't kill you. But I am gonna ask you this one time. Where is he?" Lawson took a step towards Steve. Moses gave Lawson the side-eye. Steve replied, "I don't know exactly. He rode off down that way, I imagine y'all be meeting up again real soon if you follow." He pointed towards the right side of the path. "That boy's got the engine magic all around him, be best if y'all left him alone." Law did not answer Steve's statement. He simply turned and walked away to mount his horse but Steve grabbed Moses by the shoulder before he could do the same. "Son you need to get out of here like today if you wanna live, he don't give a fuck about out you." Steve said. Moses thought for a second, looking down at the ground then rose his chin up to speak. He gestured around him. "This ain't me old man, farming and breaking my back every day for what?" He scoffed. "No fine linen, no expensive whores...this is my life." He put a hand on his gun. "The outlaw life." Steve looked at him for a moment, shook his head and replied, "That outlaw life is a short one filled with quick pleasures and a quick death."

Law spoke, "There's only one Engine I know with that much power, and I know the whore personally that is his best friend. Come Moses, we got a brothel to burn." The two rode off in the dusk as the Sun set and the stars came out to play.

Meanwhile, Justice lay in a grassy patch next to Liberty. His face was turned up to the sky as he was finally taking a rest from the events of the day. "Liberty, you think that man's soul, I mean his abilities, are in me?" he said. Liberty laid on her side, quiet and peaceful. A bat zoomed overhead making a screeching noise. Justice leaned up and pulled Betsy from Liberty's side. He took aim with nothing but the moonlight and and fired. The bat dropped right from the sky and Justice smiled and said one word, "Dinner."

Maggie did her last walk through of the brothel. Everything was packed and by morning she would be long-gone no one the wiser. It was pitch black outside. Lin Su was upstairs when Maggie heard a crash. "Lin?" she whispered, her eyes widening. A cold breeze swept through the room and Maggie backed into a corner. Deep down she already knew who was here. In the shadow corner appeared large white eyes and big sharp white teeth, the rest of the figure was completely black. A hand then reached out in leather black gloves and wrapped a hand around Maggie's mouth before she could scream. Moses whispered to her as he held a shiny knife right where her eyes could get a close view, "Scream and I'm gonna carve you up. I don't like hurting women, so please don't make me."

Law appeared at the top of the steps and started walking slowly down the stairs while loading up his pistol and spinning the revolver. Maggie's eyes watered and she asked about Lin. Law replied, "Taking a nap, but this, see this is just between me and you." He smirked. "You see, I got a problem. This east coast tender foot is killing my gang by himself and I don't know how. Then I got a little information this afternoon he's gotten some engine mambo jumbo magic about him." He laughed and threw his head back before turning to look back at her, settling in a menacing silence. "Now their is only one Engine I know in these parts where that mumbo jumbo magic is worth a damn and can be found. And I know for a fact the source comes from your good friend. So now I'm guessing you're the one who introduced them two. That sound 'bout right Moses?" "That sounds 'bout right Law." Maggie spoke calmly, "I don't know what you're talking about." "Really!" Law sneered. "Well Maggie, where you off to? Sure is dark and empty in here. Taking a vacation without me?" Maggie started to cry. "It's over, Paul." Law looked at the ground sucked his teeth the replied, "You're right. It is. So Maggie I'm a ask you one more time, did you help Jeremiah Justice kill my gang?" Maggie whimpered, "I never heard of him." "OK, well shit. Moses let's go." The two walked away and Maggie was astonished, she thought she was dead for sure. However just as they got to the door Law turned and said, "Maggie, just one thing. Whose are these?" He held Justice's spectacles in his hand. He had left them on the dresser next to his bed. This was a knife in

Maggie's heart. She gasped a frog in her throat because all she could do was tremble as Paul Lawson walked closer and Moses turned away. Screams and shrieks took over the night but no one came to the young woman's aid.

Justice awoke in a sweat, he reached for his pistol and looked in both directions. No one was in either direction except Liberty laying on her side looking at him perplexed. Justice had a bad feeling about something. Maggie came to his thoughts. She said she was leaving town for good and he had a sudden desperate urge to see her before she left. He had never been good with women, but things were different with Maggie. He freshened up with a canteen of water and a comb and was off. He reached the bordello in about two hours while thinking the whole time about what he would say. Instead of knocking, he opened the door and walked right in past the carriage which was fully loaded. Maggie sat on a piano bench next to Lin who was rubbing her back. Maggie turned and looked at Justice, one eye blood red from an exploded blood vessel and the other eye black and blue. Thumb prints were all about her neck, but her expression of defeat was the worst of all. "What you doin' here Jeremiah?" she asked. Justice put his hand over his mouth in horror. "Maggie!" Maggie inhaled sharply and looked away. "Yeah, I had this coming I suppose. Look son, you need to get out of this state like today." Justice's face grew grim. A different type of anger started to blossom in his spirit and it showed through his darkening eyes. "Where are they?" he asked quietly. Maggie sighed. "Leave it alone, Jeremiah." Justice asked again. "Where is he?" Maggie almost smiled then replied, "He left a message for you to meet him at the Old Apache Grave, but Jeremiah I wa....." Justice came face-to-face with her and stopped her short. "Maggie, leave now. I'm ending this." He kissed her on her swollen lips slowly and softly as not to hurt them and turned and walked away. Maggie and Lin were in disbelief. This was not the boy they had nurtured back to health. This was a man hardened with a mission and a destiny.

CHAPTER 8

Justice crept through a narrow rock pass, its orange stone walls were high enough to kiss the sky. The castle corridor seemed to be developed by God and had rainbows burned into its hue but Liberty knew it was a trap as stones stacked upon each other burying the dead and skulls of wolves were placed above fallen warriors. The narrow passage opened up to a circular enclosure, a sacred place cursing the unworthy. A harmonica broke the dead's slumber so that Justice's eyes shot to its origin. Moses stood a high playing his cold and sad theme. Justice thought of taking him out now while he was out in the open in his arrogance. He knew the young man's answer already, but he was still gonna ask. "Moses Freemon! You're under arrest for murder, robbery, and a slew of other crimes. Come with me and I'll see you get a fair trial."

Moses stopped playing then spoke quietly with the harmonica in his hands as he leaned against the stone wall with his feet crossed. "Why do that when we got a judge, jury and executioner right here?" He then put his head back down as he ducked behind his hat and kept playing. Justice's mind was fearful, but his heart burned with fire as if a sword was being forged. He leaped off of Liberty and gave her a smack on the rear and she disappeared so it was just the two now. "Got you some engine magic huh?" ,said Moses. Justice flinched but he said nothing. Moses continued, "Yeah good stuff, they say in this burial ground that any that are unworthy warriors will be buried here so that their souls will be tormented forever in the afterlife." Moses looked up now, an unmistakable glint in his eyes. "Are you worthy, Jeremiah? "Justice replied, "It's Justice, and yes I am worthy." Moses smirked and then continued on with his tune. "Moses, Paul don't give a damn about you. That's why he ain't come himself so don't be his fool." Moses replied, "Working back breaking day after back breaking day... and for what? Helping someone else get rich while being treated like a boy, no sir." He spread his arms out. "This... this is it for me! My name known, respected, feared. This Outlaw life is the life for me, making money, fuckin hoes. "Justice looked at him with sadness then replied, "Living with honor having a name of honor, dying old with your grand kids. Now that's a good life." Moses sniffed, stood up tall and put his harmonica away, "Not for me it isn't. Not for me, ready to die." He fixed the young boy with a steely gaze. "Justice?"

"You can't just think you're fast. You gotta know it, gotta test yourself cuz they gonna test you when your gun goes warm." Moses walked towards the edge of the cliff. "See Jeremiah, some are born for this and others like....." In the middle of Moses' speech Justice took aim and fired. The bullet hit the back of the wall and Moses was already in mid-air firing his two skull handled pistols. Justice could barely see Moses' silhouette in the blazing Sun. Take aim and fire he thought. No, roll for cover! Bullets landed in his old spot as the Murderous Moor landed running through the sacred mounds firing. Justice fired back from the cover of the stone graves but the

the well-dressed demon was a blur. Moses was firing rapidly and flicking the hammer of his pistol then switching to another gun while Justice was pinned. Moses reloaded his guns and taunted, "I'll give it to you J.J. You got heart but no brains, soon to be literally. HeHeHeeeee!" Moses spun his revolver barrel, while Justice took out a stick of dynamite and lit it. He launched it at his target, however Moses fired at the dynamite and it exploded in mid air. "Seen that trick before Marshall!" Justice couldn't even lift his head from behind the mound let alone take aim.

Moses holstered all his guns, and stood straight up walking towards Justice at a leisurely pace. "You're not even trying J.J." Lightning shot through Justice's eyes as he exposed himself just enough to take aim. Time slowed for him as the dust was flying up past his pistol's line of sight. He saw an eagle gliding slowly up above before he fired. The bullet whizzed by Moses as he side-stepped and fired from the his hip. The round struck the stone right in front of Jeremiah. Justice coiled back down as Moses laughed like a wild hyena. Justice knew there was no hope. He was just gonna get picked off. There was only one way he could possibly survive this battle. "Moses!" he shouted, sweat dripping down his face. "Moses, I challenge you to a duel." "Shit, you serious? I ain't had a duel in months." Moses said. They both stood up and approached each other about twenty yards apart. Justice had no choice. It was the end now. Moses was all around faster, but maybe if he truly believed. He held out for hope. "I'll tell you what, son. It's on you, you draw whenever you're ready." Moses said. Justice inhaled the dry air in his lungs and knew that the breaths he took now may very well be his last. Then his eyes met Moses who was big and wide like a lion and black like the night sky. His smirk infuriated Justice, but the young man calmed himself. He cleared his mind as everything settled into a thick quiet.

Moses heard a click and quickly removed his pistol from its holster and fired. A Native American dropped from the cliff above with his rifle before Justice even knew what had happened. Then they came with faces painted and with hatchets and clubs. Two came to crush his skull as a white man's scalp was the highest prize. Justice ducked the first blow and returned the favor with a shot to the kidney then removed his pistol and butted the man on the back of his skull and he fell silent. The second came with a knife to his stomach and he side-stepped this attack before grabbing the knife with one hand and landing a devastating blow on the warrior's face with his gun. Moses was not so merciful. Five warriors came for him like a pack of wolves. The closest man got a bullet right in his heart and fell to sleep with his fathers. The second received a bullet in his thigh. He went to grab his wound in pain but Moses grabbed him in a choke hold and used him as a shield. One warrior came from the front next but slowed when he saw his brother in arms as a hostage. Moses showed no remorse and landed three shots right in his chest. He twirled his pistol then holstered it. Another came from behind as the warrior raised his axe for a strike. Moses threw his shield into his path then unleashed his other two pistols and unloaded both of them so that they fell together as brothers.

A female warrior took aim at Moses in the

distance. He ducked and ran low towards her like a cheetah as her shot missed. He grabbed her by the throat and she dropped her rifle. She took a slice at him with her dagger but missed as Moses punched her in the stomach then thew her to the ground. He took aim at her then spoke, "I don't much like killing engines or women for that matter, but it's been that type of day." A shot rang out in the valley and the warrior looked over at Justice in amazement holding a Native's rifle as Moses fell to the ground. She got up quickly and looked at him in shock as he dropped the rifle then she took off running. Justice sighed in relief and dropped to his knees. He really didn't think he was gonna make it. He collected himself and got up to leave before more Natives arrived and he heard a voice. His body went cold as he turned to see Moses. "Justice!" Moses stood up, brushing the dirt from his clothes. "Justice, you got me all dirty. Fuck!" Jeremiah froze in disbelief as Moses stood up behind him, bleeding from his shoulder. "Is that duel still on Justice? " Moses asked. Justice now realized there were tears in the man's eyes. "You know, I really thought you killed me at first." Moses said as he limped over towards Justice. "You sound disappointed." Justice replied.

Moses hung his head, sniffed then replied, "Yea I am, I'm so fucking tired Jeremiah, so tired." "Moses, give up." "Hahahahahaaaaa, you funny, Justice. Slow but funny. Come on, let's see if you quick or dead!" Jeremiah stood up, his back straighter. "I know I'm fast, Moses. I have to be" Moses smiled and nodded. He took his hand off his shoulder and readied it. Justice readied himself as well. The spirits looked down on the two men eager to see who would be joining them. The wind blew and the eagle soared and cawed as Moses drew and fired. Justice looked down then touched his stomach and beautiful red crimson was all over his hand. His pistol dropped out from his grip and he fell to his knees. "That was fast, Justice. Real fast." Moses said with a smile as his pistol was still spinning on his finger after the shot. Then Moses dropped his pistol and fell to the ground clutching his heart. Justice stood up and limped over to Moses with his last breath, extended his harmonica to Justice and said two words, "Governor's Mansion." Justice walked a couple feet away but before he could whistle for Liberty he fell to the ground.

The Governor was holding his yearly Gala so he could pander to the wealthy for votes, money, and favors. The Mansion was littered with the Lords and Ladies of the west. Governor Damen was tired of rubbing elbows and he traveled to his office upstairs. As he entered his office, his executive officer chair turned to reveal none other than Paul Lawson, who was sitting back in the wide black leather-seat while smoking a cigar. Damen shut the door behind him and locked it. "I said to meet in the basement you little bastard." Law smiled a brief moment then replied, "Governor Gerald, Octavius Damen or God for short." "What do you want Law?" Damen replied. "You know what I want... your end of the bargain held up." Damen walked slowly over to the window beside Law then spoke. "Is the rest of the Hand taken care of?"

"Yup, that young Marshall you sent was one bad-ass. Picked 'em off one by one. I wonder Gov, you did tell him to leave me alive right?" Law asked. "You're alive, aren't you?" Dame grunted. He removed a key from around his neck, threw it at Paul and said "In the desk bottom left drawer you will find a birth certificate, deed to land, and a signed document appointing you as Peter J. Washington to be my chief of staff." Law didn't move an inch at first then took a long puff of the Governor's cigar and sat up and smiled. "Peter Washington. I like that, Gov. And your famous renowned doctor... is he here?" "Paul- I mean Peter, are you ready for this operation?" Governor Damen asked. "Yes indeed I am. Let's get my new life started. I've always wanted to be a politician." "As you wish, my young apprentice. Take the back staircase to the basement and I'll have him meet you there."

In the large mansion basement there was a back room door where Paul Lawson and the renowned surgeon Dr. Eugene Elsworth spoke. "Now, just lay on the table Peter. I'm going to give you something to huff that will make you sleep and when you awake you will be a new man literally." "No!" Law said. "I have another idea. I got my own little potion I'm a take and it will keep me awake while you do your thing." "This will be painful, son." "Do it, doc and hurry my gut never lies. I got a feeling it's about to get hairy" Law said, before he pulled out a bottle of mixed with opium and cocaine. He drew out a large dose with a syringe and injected himself. His eyes rolled back in his head and he laid back attentive but lost. It wasn't the first time he had done such a thing. The good doctor cringed. This wasn't part of the plan but he started away quickly rather then have the notorious Law find out his role in the Governor's plan.

CHAPTER 9

Justice walked through the snow filled valley, his feet blistering naked in the snow. No one to help him, he was all alone. That is, until he noticed one figure who stood off in the distance. "Justice, go home!" Paul Lawson shouted. Justice looked bewildered as he was holding himself shivering in the snow. He rose his head with confidence and spoke, "I am home." Law looked back at him with an ice cold stare and said, "You're not right now, but soon you will be." With that Law removed his pistol and quickly took aim and pulled the trigger. There was a loud bang then darkness.

Justice awoke in a panic as sweat poured down his face. He touched his stomach and it was bandaged but still hurt like hell. He turned his head and saw the face of the warrior female Indian he saved. Their eyes meet but before any questions could be answered a Native man walked in the stone room, spoke to the girl and beckoned for Justice to follow outside. Justice grabbed his clothes which were neatly folded beside the bed and he got dressed. He noticed his weapons were gone. He stepped outside the doorway and was amazed to see a city of stone carved out of the mountain side. Steps abound and led to mazes of pathways and stone houses. They went to the center where many others were standing. They opened a path so that he was lead to the front where nine stone seats sat. And in those nine seats sat nine elder woman with skin like raisins. They did not blink and stared unwaveringly at Justice.

One in the center motioned for Justice to come closer. As he did, the Native warrior he saved stepped forth and her and the elders exchanged words in their language and afterwards she turned and spoke to Justice, "The Elder Women say in return for saving my life and killing the "Black Demon" you shall be sparred. But leave at once for you desecrated the great burial mound." The Native American warrior's eyes burned like fire. "But they also want to know...how did you kill the Black Demon and why?" Justice responded, "You know him huh? I have killed all the members of God's Hand. All but one finger remains and I will do this tonight. But I need my weapons back and tell them I did this by a power a man named Somebody gave me."

The young warrior girl gasped. She quickly turned to translate to the whole crowd who also gasped in disbelief. One of the men Justice knocked out earlier stepped forth and pointed at him before yelling at him in his native tongue. He was accusing Justice of lying no doubt. The man hushed immediately and stepped back on a hand raised by one of the elder women. She spoke and the Native girl translated as she did, "They say God's Hand has been a thorn in their side for sometime and if our brother Somebody has performed the Forbidden Ritual with you, you must be worthy." She raised her chin. "But white devil, you will need more than the four souls of the Hand to defeat the Law. You will need to release your fire from inside, it may have kindled but it must burn as hot as the Earth's heart to vanquish the Law."

As the Sun set the Elders begun the Fire Ritual. In the center of the village they lit a huge fire and Justice sat watching it. All the warriors danced around the fire that night and breathed on Justice's bare chest setting his soul ablaze. Justice didn't even feel the burning in his stomach from the bullet wound, he just felt rage and determination. All night till the stars came out to smile on them, all the warriors gave them their strength even the ones he knocked out earlier. And the Native warrior girl painted his face. Justice looked at her dark beautiful tiger eyes and asked, "What is your name?" She replied, "I am called Crying Star. Come, it is time." She handed him his weapons back. "Here are your weapons and we will give you a horse." Justice replied, "I already have one." He stuck his fingers in his mouth and whistled. In a few moments, Liberty was heard in the distance galloping towards the city and up the steps.

Teddy and the rest of the marshals arrived at the Governor's Mansion when evening settled. They came in through the back and Governor Damen came out right away to meet them. "Good work men. I am very sorry for the loss of your friend William but there is some good news. I have the last member of God's Hand in my basement tied up." Teddy as well as the other marshals looked at each other bewildered. "The last member." Teddy repeated slowly.

"Yes, you killed all the rest. My eyes and ears are everywhere." Governor Dame replied. "I will go and retrieve him in his chains to parade in front of all my guests then I shall deliver him to you. But men, I feel it is best he doesn't make it to court would you agree?" The Governor turned and walked away and Patrick approached Teddy, "What the hell is going on? The entire Hand is dead but one?" Teddy replied, "I don't know either but if somebody gift wrapped this thing for us boys...let's take it."

The Governor and his two guards walked down the basement steps and then into the back room where Paul Lawson laid on a metal table hands with his feet tied and a bandage around his entire face except his eyes. "Doctor, you didn't have to perform the surgery. Just put him to sleep and bind him."

101

Dame sighed. "Doctor, where are you?" Dame turned to look. Soon, he and his men searched to see where the Doctor was. Just then Law arose shrugging off his fake bindings and brandishing two large bowie knives from his back in a flash. One sliced the neck of one of the Governor's guards and the other in the heart. The crimson blood spread all over the walls now with Law's blood on the floor. The Governor turned in horror to meet eyes with the Law.

"Paul, calm yourself. You still need me. we can make a deal." Dame said slowly. "A deal with you, Governor Demon? I think there will be no more deals." Law replied quietly. The Governor knew his entire plan was unraveling before his eyes. Stealing funds and eliminating competition via the God's Hand Gang. And he was so close to a Presidential bid. "Law, it's no different from what you did to your gang, but you still need me if you want to get in politics." Law sneered at this. "No, I think you've taught me all I need to know about politics. I'll take it from here."

With that, Law put his two blades to Governor Damen's neck and he gave his last reply trembling but in anger. "Paul Lawson you are an illiterate pompous popper from a long line of illiterate pompous poppers. You will never succeed in the ranks of high society because you weren't meant to live in the ranks of high society. That is why I could not bring you in, your ambitions outweigh you boy. Don't blame me, blame God!" "Yea well, this is America and in America we live by the Law. Here God is dead!" Law shouted, his eyes bulging in anger. With a clean swipe of his two blades, Law opened Damen's throat. Damen fell to his knees as the blood burst forth in the air as if one had struck oil in the soils of Texas. The whistling sound of a flute was only stopped by Damen, who grabbed his opened wound and looked at Law in amazement before he fell to the ground quick no more.

CHAPTER 10

Crying Star and Justice ended their journey on a hillside overlooking the Mansion. "We are here. Justice Devil, have faith. The ancestors guide you!" Crying Star said, her painted in the style of a messenger. Red base, black eye shade, with white tear lines. "It's just Justice." Justice replied. "I like my way better," she grinned.. Justice laughed at this and nodded. "Fair enough. Goodbye Crying Star. Thank you for everything you've done." Ancestors guide you, Justice Devil!" Crying Star said softly once again as she and her horse turned and disappeared in the night. Justice's eyes burned like as a forest struck by lightening. This was to end now. His adopted father's death would be avenged tonight.

The Marshals were getting restless looking at the guests drinking their wine and conversing not knowing a wick burned underneath their feet. "He's been gone a while now, Teddy. Maybe we should check on him." Patrick said. Teddy replied, "Maybe you're right. We..." Boom! The explosion emanated from the parlor room floor sending two guests flying through the air. The shock wave rocked all the attendees but before anyone could react a second explosion sounded in the dining room floor. Screams and cries echoed throughout, smoke filled hallways and rooms with people running for the nearest exit. Paul Lawson or rather Peter Washington whistled to the screams as he emptied the dearly deceased Governor's safe into his satchel, collected his forged documents, and headed for the door. He took one last swig of the Governor's whiskey then slammed the bottle against the wall, struck a match and lit the room a blaze the same way he did in the attic and basement.

The Marshals stayed in as long as they could evacuating the guests but the smoke was too much. When they exited the building this time the entire roof was engulfed in flames. The house went up so quick they couldn't believe it. The servants ran for water and rung the bell but it was too late. Law kicked the door open to the ballroom balcony to admire his handy work. The flames crawled up the walls like caterpillars till they ate at the ceiling. Law would burn down the old and start anew if society would not accept him. He would take his rightful place by force and he had all he needed now. Money, a good name, and a new face. It was a new day except for a familiar tune that played in the background. Law's smile quickly turned to disbelief as his eyes fixed on the figure that sat on the opposite side of the ballroom and in the balcony. Justice, Jeremiah Justice or what used to be, with his face painted black with red stripes the symbol of a new warrior. He stood and walked slowly down playing a familiar tune from the mind of Law's old friend. "Didn't think you'd make it J.J. Got some new friends, I see." Law said. "You seem to be out of friends, Law." Justice replied. He then put his head back down and continued playing. Law rolled his eyes then spoke, "Boy you really think you justice. Let me tell you what you are. You're a vigilante, a criminal and no different than me. Why don't you take some of this money here and help me fix this state? Hell, this country." Justice stopped playing, stood up straight and said, "Paul Lawson, I'm placing you under arrest by the powers vested in me by the Governor of New Palestine for murder, robbery, and a slew other offensives." Law dropped his large satchel of money, put his hands on his hips and spoke. "You know you saved me a lot of trouble taking down the gang, thought I was gonna have to pluck off two of them in the dark. You see, me and your dear dearly departed Governor had a deal. I take down his competition and in the end I get brought into the fold with a new face and identity."

Justice said nothing but kept playing while Law spoke, "I didn't think you'd get past old Moses though, but Justice I'm a whole other kind of demon. You see Jeremiah Justice, there is a difference between Justice and the Law. The law is fact." Lawson cleared his throat and glanced up at the sky as if recalling something important. He spoke lightly. "Fact: to be poor in America is a death sentence. Fact: the only way to get ahead is by taking what you want. Fact: certain people belong in certain places.

Fact: America was built on murder, backstabbing, and lies, and if you ain't ready to do that then get the fuck out the way or get slaughtered with the rest of the hogs. Fact...Justice is an illusion! " Lawson finished these last words with an angry shout. He paced forward, reaching for his pistol. "Fact: you better stop playing that fucking harmonica!" He grabbed his pistol and jumped onto the balcony railing. Justice in a flash had the harmonica in his pocket and leaped on the same railing and fired in Law's direction. The two ran on the railing in opposite directions like cats and throwing lightning at one another like gods. Justice dove through the air as steel whizzed past his head. He aimed and had Law clear in his sight. The round hit the statue that Law took cover behind. Justice hit the ground and did the same. "It's not enough Justice!" Law said reloading his pistols." "What type of law you live by, Paul? Get the only family you ever had killed for what?" Justice asked.

"Money, power, respect in that order. What you think, the men you work for ain't criminals?" Law shouted. He lit a cigarette and put it in his mouth.

The toxins he took earlier were in full effect but his face was in dire pain still. He grabbed one of the last five sticks of dynamite from his coat and lit it. Jeremiah knew this game. He grabbed a cigarette and did the same grabbing a stick from his back waist. The two sticks of dynamite flew past each other in the air landing in the two knight's paths. They ran as explosions blew behind them. They fired frantically, the bullets were all over the place as the ceiling fell above them. Justice was coming to the end of the balcony to where he would have met Law and he saw it. Law's bag of money. He only had one stick as Law's final stick landed just behind his feet. He dove over the railing with his sights set on the duffel bag. The dynamite stick landed directly in it. Law slid to his backside stopping as the explosion shredded the bag and money into confetti as Justice went crashing through the table.

Law screamed in horror as his money fell before him as snow and ash. Foaming behind his bloody bandage wraps, Law spotted Justice who was injured in between the broken table. He holstered his pistol and removed his daggers, leaping off the railing screaming with flames behind him. "JUSTICE!" Jeremiah stumbled crawling on the floor when he saw Law coming at him like Satan himself. He removed his machete from his back like a shinobi and deflected Law's attack. He came to his balance quickly and parried all of Laws wild spinning blows with ease. A lunge by Law missed its mark and it was a clean opening for Justice. With a swipe he cut Law's thigh and mad him stumble. Law was furious. He let out a howl and charged. Windmill strike after strike, Justice blocked them and a powerful slash connecting with Law's daggers left another opening as he stumbled back. Justice did a spinning strike and sliced Law's stomach. A gush of blood spattered onto the floor. Justice did a double mariachi stomp after and sheathed his blade.

Law limped away like a wounded animal in fear when his eyes caught an angel for a gift. He saw a servant damsel running for her life. He angled the straggler and cut her off. She screamed in terror as he grabbed her in one arm and put his pistol to her head with the other. Law yelled out, "Drop the gun Justice or this bitch gets it." Justice said nothing just kept Law in his sights with his pistol. Justice fired so a spark hit and Law's pistol flew out his hand. Law howled in pain, grabbing his wrist. The woman ran for her life. Justice twirled his pistol and holstered it before he spoke, "It's over Law, don't make me do this." Law bent over holding his stomach. "Think you're faster than me, Justice? Let's find out."

The two stood firm and a few yards apart as the roof fell down around them. There were but seconds left. Law looked directly in Justice's eyes and felt a chill go over him. He was so close, was this it? He was in a corner and then it happened. Teddy kicked in the doors yelling, "Is anyone still here?" Teddy didn't even see Law right next to him but instead fixed his gaze on Justice in amazement. "J.J. did you do this?" he asked. "What's all over your face, you've gone savage out there didn't ya? Did you do this?"Before Justice could answer Teddy rushed him and put him in a headlock trying to drag him out. Law smiled. This was too good to be true. No, he thought. This was destiny. Justice and his eyes met again. The smile seen through the bandages was too much. Justice flipped Teddy over with a slam. Teddy fell on the floor with a loud and heavy crash. Law was enjoying this farce, but it was time. He went for his gun. Teddy's face was covered in blood by the time Justice stopped hitting him and looked up at Lawson.

There were only two decisions to make and time was not on Justice's side. Justice grabbed Teddy by his coat and pulled him in so the both of them rolled behind a pillar for cover. Law ran towards the window firing at the two other men, but Justice pulled Teddy around the pillar rotating for cover. Law went crashing through a side window head first as the building crumbled behind him. Justice wanted to follow him. He looked down at Teddy who didn't even know where he was anymore. Justice carried him over his shoulder to the main hallway when Teddy spoke. "Stop, stop. Jeremiah, I'm okay. Go follow him." Justice didn't know what to say, he felt bad now for flipping Teddy over. "Are you sure?" he asked. "Yes... go!" Justice let him go, looked at him one last time in the eyes then ran through the smoke to follow Law. Teddy turned in disgust and limped out the front door as Patrick came to great him. "Ted, what happened in there?" Patrick asked. "J.J.

He snuck me he's gone savage in war paint, he lit the place on fire. I think he killed the Governor." "What? And Law?" Patrick asked. "No sign probably dead." Teddy replied. Teddy's face grew grim as he turned and watched the mansion cave in from the flames. His pride had taken a mighty blow and Justice would pay.

Two weeks later, Peter Washington walked up the stairs to the Supreme Court of New Palestine's Judge's chambers. Peter knocked then entered a room filled with Senators, Judges, and other high ranking officials. "This is the young man that was Governor Damen's chief of staff?" Senator Casey asked. "Yes I am." Peter replied. "I was newly appointed and hand picked by the Governor. We were planning great things." "Yes..." replied Senator Casey. "I've read the Governor's letter here about you. Harvard, top of class. Your father died in the war." "Yes, Governor Damen was like a new found father to me. We... excuse me I'm still a little shaken up still." Peter sighed. "It's fine, son. We all are. Now it looks as if you have what it takes plus being the Governor's apprentice is a nice platform, but we need you to follow our wishes if you want to succeed. Can you do that?" Senator Casey asked smiling. Peter almost smiled back then spoke. "I think I know the law of the land quite well sir." The old men and their new found prized pet poured wine and lit cigars as they discussed Peter Washington's future.

On an old dusty trail Justice took a sip of his canteen on top of Liberty and unfolded a piece of paper. It read, "Jeremiah Justice Wanted for Murder of Governor Damen." Justice patted Liberty on her side and said, "It's okay, girl. Just remember in America Justice eventually comes for us all." He then gave his reigns a whip and they galloped off in the back open plane, with distant mountains, clouds asunder and the sun all smiling down on Justice and Liberty.

POSTFACE

To this the end, I hope none have ill will towards this piece. I merely wished to ask the question of what is the difference between justice and the law? Not just at face value but in even deeper terms. What is the law of the outlaw if there is one? In Romans 13:1 it is written: "Let every person be subject to the governing authorities. For there is no authority except from God, and those that exists have been instituted by God. " But what about men of the law who have become corrupt for they are but men. How does a man of the law seek justice when the law skews, prevents, and perverts justice. Is there a difference between justice and the law? I say yes, so what should we do then? Seek our own forms of justice - street justice, as it were? I battle with the thought almost daily as I see innocent friends slain and yet constantly culprits and outlaws go unpunished. Yes the wheels of justice turn very, very slowly. But in the end justice catches up with us all, maybe not in this story but surely in the next. To the men and women of this story and many other stories they all had their chance to make a change. However they did not. No matter what your reasons for doing wrong, we all must deal with the consequences. Even if we told ourselves this was for family, just a little while until I have enough. We may tell ourselves this is for the greater good or even fuck it, I am one with the darkness. However, we all must deal with the wrath of justice. I bid you farewell until the next story and thank you for your time which is worth more than money.

Poetically, Jim Denson